ME AND ORSON WELLES

Robert Kaplow is a teacher and writer who for over fifteen years has written satirical songs and sketches for National Public Radio's *Morning Edition*, where he created 'Moe Moskowitz and the Punsters.' His acclaimed young adult novels include *Alessandra in Love* and *Alex Icicle: A Romance in Ten Torrid Chapters*. He is also the other author of two literary satires: *The Cat Who Killed Lilian Jackson Braun* and *Who's Killing the Great Writers of America?*

OTHER WORKS BY ROBERT KAPLOW

The Cat Who Killed Lilian Jackson Braun
Who's Killing the Great Writers of America?

ROBERT KAPLOW

Me and Orson Welles

VINTAGE BOOKS
London

Published by Vintage 2009

2 4 6 8 10 9 7 5 3 1

First published in the United States of America by MacAdam/Cage in
2003

Vintage
Random House, 20 Vauxhall Bridge Road,
London SW1V 2SA

www.vintage-books.co.uk

Addresses for companies within The Random House Group Limited
can be found at: www.randomhouse.co.uk/offices.htm

The Random House Group Limited Reg. No. 954009

A CIP catalogue record for this book
is available from the British Library

ISBN 9780099540199

The Random House Group Limited supports The Forest
Stewardship Council (FSC), the leading international forest
certification organisation. All our titles that are printed on
Greenpeace approved FSC certified paper carry the FSC logo.
Our paper procurement policy can be found at:
www.rbooks.co.uk/environment

Printed in the UK by CPI Bookmarque, Croydon, CR0 4TD

to my father Jerome

Me and Orson Welles is a work of fiction. Although it is set against a background of real persons and historical events, those persons and events have been substantially reimagined in the storytelling.

Special thanks to Arthur Anderson and Samuel Leve of the 1937 Mercury Theatre production of *Julius Caesar* for the hours they spent talking to me.—R.K.

Saturday, November 6
One

This is the story of one week in my life. I was seventeen. It was the week I slept in Orson Welles's pajamas. It was the week I fell in love. It was the week I fell out of love. And it was the week I changed my middle name—twice.

My memory of that period is of things *happening*—almost without cease. There must be a remarkable time in everybody's life when the phone doesn't stop ringing—when the mailman brings you nothing but success—when you walk down the street, the sunlight pouring around you, scarcely able to believe your own good luck.

That Saturday morning the phone was ringing again. My grandfather's Model A was pulling up in front of the house. The living-room radio was blaring news about the Japanese invading China.

On the second floor, my sister was playing her Crosby record of "The Moon Got in My Eyes" for the eight-millionth time. It was the latest in a series of sentimental ballads that served as emotional chapter titles to what I imagined was her overdreamed and underlived life.

"Change the needle!" I said as I headed toward the bathroom. "You're wrecking it."

"Twerp."

"Another county heard from." This from my mother. She was knocking spiderwebs from the ceiling with a broom. "Your father works every day 'til nine o'clock at night, and now on Saturday he has to rake leaves yet? You *enjoy* giving him more work?"

I went into my Paul Muni impersonation from *The Life of Emile Zola*: "The day will come when France will *thank* me...for having helped to save her *honor!*" (Voice breaking huskily on *honor* to simulate overwhelming emotion.)

"It's no use."

"What's he shouting for, Nutsy Fagen?" This from my grandmother downstairs.

I checked my reflection in the hall mirror. Not bad, I thought. Sometimes I really did look like *somebody*—a writer, an actor—the earnestness of Gary Cooper, the playfulness of Cary Grant, and maybe just a whisper of Astaire. I struck an Astaire-like pose, straightened an imaginary tie, and sang into the camera:

I've been a roaming Romeo,
My Juliets have been many...

Oh, I was crazy for songs that year. Knew all the verses; knew the names of all the composers and the lyricists; knew the shows and the movies they were from. I'd picked a lot of it up from my grandmother's sheet music collection, but even more I'd learned from my near-obsessive listening to the radio. (The radio and the public library were my two connections to something bigger than Westfield, New Jersey.) My parents' old Atwater Kent sat next to my bed, the hot dust from the tubes sweetening the air 'til two in the morning, filling the room with Benny Goodman's "Avalon," Mildred Bailey's "There's a Lull in My Life," Glen Gray, Ruth Etting, Isham Jones. And Saturday nights there was *Theatre News* with John Gassner—and voices in my own bedroom were talking about the new George S. Kaufman play, and Richard Rodgers himself was playing the piano, and Lorenz Hart was speaking: "Here's our first song hit, 'Manhattan,' from the *Garrick Gaieties*." And the Lunts were laughing about *Amphitryon 38*, and Harold Clurman was directing the new Clifford Odets.

I lay there at night, and I felt *close* to it all. New York City and the CBS Radio Workshop. Close enough to touch, if I could just get through the right door. Forty minutes from where I lived, Irving Berlin was writing a new song that two months from now every person in the world would be singing. All of it *vibrating* out there!

And some mornings when the light was good, and

the coffee and the Fig Newtons were scalding through
me, I'd think—at least for a few intoxicated seconds:
"You know, Richard, you can do all that, too." I wasn't
sure whether I wanted to write songs or direct plays or
write novels or maybe do everything—like the Jewish
Noel Coward.

Sheldon Coward presents Hollywood!

So I pored through the memoirs and the back issues
of *Theatre Arts Monthly* in the public library searching
for the answer. I read the biographies of every actor and
writer I admired for their secrets. How did it happen?
When did they know? What was the breakthrough?

I'd just finished Noel Coward's autobiography,
Present Indicative. I thought it was the best book I'd ever
read, and I kept comparing myself to him: O.K., Coward
was twenty-five when he wrote, directed, and starred in
The Vortex. That still gave me eight years. He wrote "A
Room with a View" when he was twenty-eight, so I still
had a little time there, too. But Berlin was only twenty-
two when he wrote "When I Lost You."

God, it was going to be hard to keep up.

Downstairs, the phone was still ringing. It was nearly
always for me; mostly the guys at school—the Black
Crow Crew we called ourselves, the seven of us, in
celebration of our drinking exploits. (Black Crow was
this toxically cheap beer we drank.) But it wasn't the
drinking that had pulled me to the Black Crow Crew. It

was the *energy* of Stefan and Skelly and the rest of them—this vanguard of good-looking male power in Westfield High School. They had a kind of celebrity glow about them that just about defined the word *desirable*. That I was permitted to be close to them seemed nothing short of a miracle. Last year, Stefan had been standing outside of study hall eyeing up this amazing tenth-grader, Kristina Stakuna. We noticed each other staring at her ass, and we both cracked up laughing. We ended up sitting next to each other in that study hall for half a year, and so became friends. It was strange, because we seemed almost opposites. Stefan was five feet tall, tough, physically intense—about once a week he got thrown out of school for beating the crap out of somebody. I was taller and significantly less imposing, an Honors English type. Sometimes, with Stefan, I felt I was the pilot fish hovering just behind the shark. I think I gave him some sort of dubious intellectual credentials—and in return I fell under his protection. Nobody could mess with me, or they'd have to deal with Stefan and the Black Crow Boys. I rewrote his entire research paper on Walt Whitman. A+, *Phil, it's great to see you finally working to your potential*. In return he set fire to Kimberley Kagan's car when she refused to go to the prom with me. It was definitely a fair trade. Of course, Skelly, Stefan, Korzun, Townsend, and the rest of them knew every beautiful girl in the school—I mean, these girls were *lining up* for the privilege of dating these guys, or even being near them, sitting in the same diner as they did on a late Saturday night. And while those particular romantic spoils hadn't yet fallen my way, just the *proximity* of beautiful women was exciting. I was sort of the approachable liaison to the Black Crow Crew. Gorgeous girls would stop and ask me if I knew whether Stefan had plans for the weekend. They were so close I could smell their perfume, could stare with perfect innocence at their impossibly lovely arms and the sculpted perfection of their stockinged legs. And, all right, I may have been invisible to them, but they weren't invisible to me. One time Kate Rouilliard looked directly at me with the cool lamps of her enormous blue eyes, and I couldn't sleep an entire week.

My grandfather was standing in front of the phonograph in the living room listening to my father's Jolson records. He was still dressed in his hat, scarf, and black Chesterfield coat with the velvet collar.

So 'til we meet again,
Heaven only knows where or when,
Think of me now and then,
Little pal!

My mother handed me the phone.
"Hi, it's Caroline."

My heart leapt a little. All right, she was short, she looked a little "librarian," but, hell, it was a start. I thought she was pretty. My affiliation with the mighty Black Crow Crew was finally beginning to pay off— although my relationship with Caroline Tice had become a sort of joke among the Boys. I'd been seeing her for two months now and hadn't even kissed her. "Pounce!" Stefan and Skelly kept yelling at me. "*Pounce* that broad. That's what she's *waiting* for you to do. Don't *ask* her, for Christ's sake."

"I'm getting there."

"He's *getting* there."

"Slowly."

"Listen," said Stefan. "Broads aren't interested in slowly. Their *parents* are interested in slowly."

Skelly was jabbing his finger in my face. He wore a white beer jacket signed with names and obscenities.

"They want you to be aggressive," he said. "They *want* you to fight for 'em."

I looked at the ground and shook my head. "I don't know if that's who I am."

Stefan nailed me. "And who you *are*—is that who you *want* to be?"

"I don't know."

At this point they usually slapped their heads in disbelief.

Even *I* sometimes slapped my head in disbelief, but

this was my enduring problem with girls. I was always the "friend" and never the "boyfriend." I shared all their romantic troubles during lunch; they showed me their diaries; I got the jubilant: "The big idiot finally *asked* me!" I got: "Richard, you're the only guy I can really *talk* to. I mean, I can talk to you like a girl." But I never got the dream, the Unhooked Capacious Brassiere. I never got the "you-can-take-off-my-stockings-before-my-parents-get-home." Which is exactly what Skelly got, and Stefan got. In abundance. Overflowing.

But I thought I had a chance with Caroline Tice. At least a slight chance. She was guileless and smart. Green Lutheran eyes. I liked her shortness; I liked her Lutheran eyes; I liked her ring size. She wore her hair as short as a guy's, and I liked that, too.

And I was polite. Oh, God, I was polite. I bought her flowers. I wrote her parents elaborate thank you notes whenever they'd had me over for dinner—sixty-hour suppers where they smiled with courteous Lutheran horror at the Fast-Talking Jew Boy their green-eyed jewel had dragged home.

"The show is at eight," Caroline was saying, "but I have to be there by at *least* six-thirty. And, Richard, please, no more rowdiness from your drunken friends."

"It wasn't us."

"It wasn't *we*."

Caroline had the lead in *Growing Pains*, which was

being performed that night for the second and final time. I'd gone the previous evening. It was a terrible play, a "comedy of youth" filled with characters named "Dutch" and "Slim" and "Spats" shrieking about roller skates and lost baseball gloves.

Anyway, the only really enjoyable moment of the play was when Kristina Stakuna (Amazon Queen of the Swollen Softballs) came onstage and the entire Black Crow Crew started stomping and giving her wolf whistles.

"That artful uplift!" called out Stefan.

Then Skelly got all seven of us singing to the tune of "That Old Feeling":

> I saw you last night,
> And got that old boner.

At the intermission Dr. Mewling invited us to leave.

We goofed around on the front steps of the school, smoking my terrible Wings cigarettes and indulging in wildly obscene fantasies about Kristina Stakuna and the college goon she was dating. "I heard when she visited him at Rutgers," said Stefan, "that he screwed her for *nine* hours straight. When he was done he had to go to the hospital. I'm not shittin' ya."

I'd met up with Caroline after the show. "That was really raw," she'd said. "You embarrassed Kristina. You embarrassed me. You guys are *really* raw." But even as she said the words, it struck me that she had actually enjoyed it—that she, too, had been briefly illuminated by the celebrity of the mighty Black Crow Crew.

"Am I going to see you this afternoon?" she asked, now on the phone. "Or are you going to drag me into New York again to look at old boarded-up theatres and say, 'Did you know Eva Le Gallienne starred in *Peter Pan* here in 1925?'"

"1926."

"Look, I'll see you tonight. And do me a favor: tell the Black Crow Crew they're officially *not* invited. Tell them they can come to the party afterwards at Kristina's house; I'm *sure* they'll enjoy that."

"I'm sure *you'd* enjoy that."

"I am *not* interested in Phil Stefan, Richard."

"Then you're the only girl in the school who isn't."

When I replaced the phone, Jolson was still wailing: *Dirty hands! Dirty face!*

"Ma!" I yelled to no one in particular. "I'm heading out."

"*Gai gezint,*" said my grandfather.

I stood by the front door wearing my father's old black double-breasted coat (too big for me, but I liked that it felt as if it were a costume from *Uncle Vanya*) and my battered black fedora—a five-dollar bill folded into my sock.

"The leaves!" called my mother.

"Tomorrow! Ma, I've got nothing on my schedule tomorrow but raking! I'm going to do seventeen, maybe eighteen hours straight."

The front door was already shutting behind me.

"It's no use," I heard her say.

Two

I walked toward the library feeling that the weights I had been lifting in the mornings were finally beginning to show some results. I'd begun working out last spring under the direction of Stefan, who assured me that I could *transform* myself into him.

How influenced I was by every encounter that came my way. I still said out loud each morning: "Every day in every way I am getting better and better"—and who the hell believed that anymore? My parents had bought me Dale Carnegie's *How to Win Friends and Influence People* and that stuff was rattling inside me, too. *Be a good listener. Encourage others to talk about themselves.*

I took a folded postcard from my wallet, and the librarian handed me a never-been-read copy of Rosamond Gilder's *John Gielgud's Hamlet*.

The immaculate newness of its shiny wrapper in my hands felt delicious. On the cover was Gielgud's hawklike profile, framed in a high black collar. There were more photographs inside, set designs, plus the entire edited scripts of Gielgud's famous 1934 and 1936 productions.

I started reading the book as I walked toward the

train station. I could hear that evocative and autumnal Saturday-morning sound: the bass drums booming from the marching band as they practiced. Some small current of guilt passed through me; I was a drummer in that band, and I should have been standing inside the fieldhouse on Rahway Avenue with the rest of them. "What the hell," I said. "Sometimes you gotta pounce."

Somebody had left a *Westfield Leader* on the train, and I skimmed it as we rattled east.

Republicans Sweep Local Vote, Win All Four Council Seats.

What was my family doing here?

My father owned United Tire Sales on Broad Street in Newark, and instead of going bust in the crash, his used-tire business had wildly flourished. Nobody could afford new tires anymore, and he had thousands of used ones stacked to the ceiling. All at once he was pulling in so much money he didn't know what to do with it. At one point we were hiding it in the oven. And in a daring gesture of social mobility (engineered by my mother, who, in her own way, was pretty courageous), we moved to our fairytale-looking Victorian house on Lawrence Avenue in Westfield, where the green-eyed Lutherans grew.

I changed trains at Newark for the Hudson Tubes, and I was trying hard to hold on to my sense of energy and optimism. I checked my reflection in the window—O.K., smooth the part in the hair, bring down the shoulders a little bit, loosen the intensity around the eyes, add just the subtlest suggestion of an ironic smile. Gable in *It Happened One Night*. Energy and maybe even a little arrogance. ("Yes, I love her, but don't hold it against me; I'm a little screwy myself.")

I held the *Hamlet* cover up to the window next to my reflection and tried to mimic Gielgud's august and severe pose. I heard my John Barrymore record in my head: *Presenting John Barrymore, crown prince of the royal family of the American theatre, as Hamlet, melancholy lover of Shakespeare's immortal drama!*

I arched my eyebrows with great dramatic intensity, pulled at my collar like the drunken wreck of a once-great stage performer, and, loudly, since nobody else was in the car, went into my Barrymore impersonation. It was an English accent that no Englishman would have found remotely recognizable. I knew the whole record by heart: "Ladies and gentlemen, I feel quite *sure* that you are all so well acquainted with this famous soliloquy from *Hamlet* that any attempt at *elucidation* on my part, other than the soliloquy itself, might be justly considered a bit of impertinence. As you remember, it goes as follows. *(Long pause)* 'To be...or not to be... *That* is the question. Whether 'tis *nobler*—'"

The ticket-taker was staring down at me.

"Just practicing," I said. "Vocal exercises."

* * *

New York was alive with rich people in Packards honking their horns at the buses, beautiful women in fur coats, panhandlers begging for a nickel, and street-vendors selling steaming ears of corn.

I bought a bag of peanuts ("A Bag a Day for More Pep") and turned up my collar against the wind. This indeed, I thought, was the figure I was born to cut—hands deep in the pockets of my enormous Russian coat, hat at a suitably Bohemian tilt, striding uptown with nothing to do but feel wonderful.

I needed a song. It was the game I played in New York, choosing my audition song for that moment when Jed Harris, leaning forward from his second-floor window, phone jammed against his ear, would cry out: "Wait a minute, Murray. You're not going to believe this, but I think our Kid just walked by!"

So far this hadn't happened.

I sang to myself "Have You Got Any Castles?" which was my favorite song at the moment. It was number five on the Hit Parade. And I was a *serious* chronicler of the Hit Parade; I listened with my notebook open, entering the top ten songs next to my neatly prenumbered list. My notebooks went back to 1935.

I walked up to the Gaiety on Broadway to look through the new sheet music. "Once in a While" was playing in the store. There was all sorts of stuff I hadn't heard yet, including some new Richard Rodgers from *I'd Rather Be Right*.

At the upright piano in the corner, trying out a new song, sat a sort of poetic-looking girl about my age. She wore wire-rim glasses and had one of those dark-haired, milk-white faces that I'm a sucker for. Every year I fell for a face like that—and they were always named Gretchen or Marian. And they'd sit in Honors English and drop references to all these books I'd never quite gotten around to reading, quoting beautiful lines of poetry right out of the air. "Doesn't Keats have a line about that?" they'd say to the teacher so quietly it was almost a private conversation. The teacher nodded and beamed, and the rest of us were thinking: "Who the hell is Keats?"

Well, she sat at the piano playing "Nice Work if You Can Get It"—so slowly it sounded like a dirge. She wore a floral vest over a large comfortable-looking lavender shirt, blue jeans, and unpolished saddle shoes. Her hair was pulled back in a George Washington.

"Swell tune," I said. I leaned against the piano, smiling with the casualness of a natural-born fraud. "And you play it with real feeling." (*Make the other person feel important—and do it sincerely.*)

"God, it's so *sad*, isn't it?" she said. "This just makes me want to *cry*."

"You could probably pick up the tempo a little bit."

"No, I mean Gershwin being *dead* and all. The fact that we'll never have another Gershwin song."

I nodded.

"No more Gershwin music—just this sort of dead air." She stopped playing. "Wouldn't that make a great title for a story—'Dead Air'?"

"Sure. I guess. I mean, well, you know, a sort of *depressing* story."

She whipped out a notepad from her back pocket and wrote down the title. The skin of her cheeks and ears was so pale you could see the veins beneath it. "Did you hear what happened to Porter?" she asked. "Had a riding accident and broke his legs? I wonder if he'll still be able to write." She stood up and massaged the small of her neck with her fingertips. "They don't like me sitting here not buying anything."

"You know so much about music, are you a songwriter?"

"I'm a real writer," she said. "Of course, Gershwin is a real writer. *Was* a real writer." Then she was putting on her coat, and the salesman was closing in on us rapaciously.

"So what do you write?" I asked. (*Talk in terms of the other person's interest.*)

She stopped and touched her neck again. From one of the booths I could hear somebody listening to "Have

You Met Miss Jones?"

"God, I like that song," she said.

"Beau-dee-ful melody," said the salesman: a short guy who looked as if someone had just poured hair tonic on his face. "There's only *one* man on earth who can write a melody like that. Rodgers. Just got copies today."

"His melodies are like lullabies, aren't they?" the girl said to me.

"Beau-dee-ful," said the salesman.

"And he knocks 'em out in ten minutes," I said. "I heard him on John Gassner."

"You listen to that, too? God, sometimes I think I'm the only one in New York who listens to that show. Can you imagine just sitting down and coming up with the melody to 'Small Hotel'?"

"We got 'Small Hotel'!" said the salesman. "Ten weeks on the Hit Parade. Couldn't keep it in the store." He was wildly trying to locate a copy on the wall. "People came in. Didn't even ask what they wanted. Just handed them a copy."

"I'd give my *blood* to write any five notes as beautiful as the first five notes to 'Small Hotel,'" she said.

"What *do* you write, uh—"

"Gretta. I haven't written anything very *significant* yet," she said. "Actually, I'm trying to write a play."

"A play? Wow. That's interesting, because I'm a sort of actor."

"Really? What have you done?"

"Oh," I said, "you know, Federal Theatre mostly. *It Can't Happen Here…Injunction Granted…*the Voodoo *Macbeth.*"

She smiled at my lunatic catalogue of lies. "I thought the Voodoo *Macbeth* had an all-Negro cast."

"Well, I stood in the shadows most of the time. So you're really a writer, Gretta?" (*Remember that a man's name is to him the sweetest and most important sound in any language.*)

"I wish I could convince the *New Yorker* of that. And then my parents. And then myself. Actually, I'd skip my parents and myself, if I could just convince the *New Yorker.* Did you read the John Cheever piece about his childhood maid? God, that was so beautiful. And so *quiet,* you know? Just this small miracle. Have you gone to the *Times* bookfair yet? Don't. It's lousy. And so crowded. I gotta go, uh—"

"Richard," I said. "Do you want to have—"

"Good luck with your acting. Wouldn't this make a great scene for a story?" she said. "Just two people meeting like this? Nothing more. It's just so New York."

Later that afternoon I took a bus downtown to the library. I thought maybe I'd read some plays.

I studied the piece of sheet music I'd bought: "Have

You Met Miss Jones?" Sam H. Harris presents Geo. M. Cohan in the new musical comedy *I'd Rather Be Right*. Book by Geo. S. Kaufman and Moss Hart. Lyrics by Lorenz Hart. Music by Richard Rodgers.

The electricity of those names! They radiated a kind of *significance*. Kaufman...Hart...Rodgers. And they walked the same streets I did.

The bus stopped at 42nd Street in front of the library, and I noticed a little action down beyond Bryant Park. I walked toward Sixth, and there on West 41st Street was a truck, a ladder, and a group of people standing outside a theatre.

Three

On the side of the theatre, painted on the brick wall, an old sign still read Comedy Theatre, but a new electrical sign was being bolted into the brickwork at the center of the building. Its wires trailed through the third-floor window.

A dozen people stood outside. Nearly all of them looked to be in their twenties.

"Wait a second! Wait a second!" yelled a hatless guy with curly sand-colored hair. He was calling up to the electrician. "Don't do anything 'til I come back."

The guy on the ladder called down, "I shouldn't be doing this on the Sabbath. The Talmud says—"

Everybody groaned.

"Thus spake the Rabbi," said a heavy-set young man with a British accent. He leaned a foot on the fire hydrant in front of the theatre. He was dressed in an expensive-looking coat, and, clearly, he was in charge. Next to him stood a young woman holding a clipboard. She was hardly older than I was. She wore no coat: a gray sweater with its sleeves pulled back. College, I thought. Below the sweater she wore—long and loose—a brown and gray tweed skirt. The stitched collar of the sweater

was highlighted by a string of pearls. Her face was round,
shadowed—the eyes dark, sharp, staring down at the
ground in thought. Her chestnut hair was parted exactly
in the middle and then pulled back tightly. Running
from behind her ears, around the top of her head, almost
like a tiny garland, was a hairband designed to resemble
a slender braid of chestnut hair. I thought: How could
one city be filled with so many striking women?

She looked up suddenly, right at me—took my
measure, smiled—then returned her gaze downward.

My blood pulsed.

"Will somebody go find Orson?" said the man with
the British accent.

There came the sound of jackhammering down the
street—and then there was an ambulance, lights
flashing, pulling up in front of the theatre. No one
seemed to notice it.

One of the lobby doors opened and the curly-headed
guy ran out carrying a snare drum on a stand. "Wait!
Don't start 'til I get this set up." He was like a one-man
Three Stooges trying to set up the drum kit. The cymbal
went rolling down the sidewalk. I caught it. He
tentatively hit the drum a few times, then spoke into the
drumstick. "Good evening, ladies and gentlemen, this is
Ben Bernie and all the lads coming to you live from the
beautiful Derelict Theatre on West 41st Street—
yowzah!"

"Sonja, will you tell Orson to get *out* here?" said the British gentleman. He sneezed, then wiped his nose with his handkerchief.

"Difficult to tell Orson anything," said the girl.

Somebody said, "Tell him there's a dozen young, well-toned ballerinas out here. That'll get him out."

People laughed.

I watched as she pushed open the theatre door.

"Well, *she'll* be gone for an hour."

"Steady, lads," said the British gentleman.

A delivery truck pulled up behind the ambulance. The driver dragged out some cardboard boxes. Attached to the top of each box was a sample of what was inside— a flier printed in blood-red letters on yellow paper.

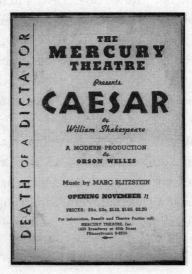

"Notice there's no date for the opening."

"At least we're opening in *November.*"

As the British gentleman signed for the boxes, the curly-headed guy was still trying unsuccessfully to play a drumroll. Somebody else tried, too—also terribly.

"This is the best drumroll the Mercury Theatre can come up with?" asked the British gentleman.

"It's the best we can do with a nonunion drummer. Comes the revolution—"

"Strike! Strike!"

"All ready up here!" called the little man on the ladder. He had climbed into the third-floor window. "Later I'll wire you a switch. Now I'll just plug it in."

"Will someone *please* get Orson!"

"Vakhtangov!" somebody cried. Then the cry was picked up by the others. "Vakhtangov! Vakhtangov!"

A poor skinny guy in a massively wrinkled white shirt headed into the theatre, tripping over the doorjamb.

"I'm going to plug it in," said the little man in the window.

"Wait! Wait!"

They were still fumbling with the drumroll—and with a kind of crazy boldness and a sense of *What the hell do I have to lose?* I said to the curly-haired guy, "Give me the sticks. I'll do it."

"What?"

"I said I'll play you a drumroll."

"Oh, yeah? And who are you?"

"I'm Gene Krupa. Who are you?"

"'Truly, my name is Cinna. I'm Cinna the poet.'"

Then there was laughter, and instantly about five of them were doing a scene.

"'Where do you dwell?'"

"'In the Capital.'"

"'Whither are you going?'"

"'I'm going to Caesar's funeral.'"

"'His name's Cinna.'"

"'Tear him for his bad verses!'"

"Tear him for his bad drumming!"

The little man at the third-floor window called out: "I'm going to plug it in!"

I sizzled into a killer drumroll on the snare. The Westfield High School marching band had never heard one better. Possibly all of America had never heard one better. The drumroll alone got me a hand from the crowd.

"Swell!" the curly-haired guy said. He wagged his forefinger and started truckin'. "Peel the Big Apple, kid!"

"Tear him for his bad dancing!"

I thought of Stefan's words: And who you *are*—is that who you *want* to be?

And I answered him: *Starting today it is.*

The double doors of the theatre entrance flew back, and a young man emerged swearing loudly in an astonishingly deep and resonant voice. "Goddamn-sons-of-bitches! Is every *single* person in this show against me? Is this a goddamn *conspiracy* to wreck my show?"

It was Orson Welles. At twenty he had starred on Broadway in *Romeo and Juliet*. At twenty-one he had directed *Macbeth* for the Negro Theatre in Harlem—transforming the witches into witch doctors and setting the play in Haiti. Later that year he'd directed and starred in *Doctor Faustus*—then marched an entire audience to an empty theatre uptown when the federal government had locked out his production of *The Cradle Will Rock*. I'd heard that now he was forming his own classical repertory company on Broadway. He was to be the director, the producer, the star.

He was twenty-two years old.

Five years older than I was.

He held a bound script in his black-gloved hands, and he wore a blue pinstriped suit under an open overcoat. Sonja and Vakhtangov followed in his wake.

The British gentleman—who by now I figured out was John Houseman—handed Welles one of the newly printed fliers.

"This is completely inadequate," said Welles. "Very possibly the worst-looking thing I've ever seen in my life."

"We just had two hundred thousand of them printed."

"They're not *entirely* bad," said Welles, then he wheeled on me. "Can you play the ukulele?"

I looked up into the round boyish face from which that amazing voice issued. "Sure," I said. I figured how hard could it be? It only had four strings. I kept the drumroll going. (*Talk in terms of the other man's interest.*) "Mr. Welles, if you need somebody to play the ukulele, you couldn't find anybody in this city better than I am."

"The kid's got balls. Will you work for nothing?"

"*Orson—*" Houseman said.

"Quiet! I'm *negotiating.*" He saw the copy of *John Gielgud's Hamlet* that I had jammed under my arm, and he pulled it out. He frowned at the cover photograph. "Have you ever heard anybody so in love with the sound of his own goddamn voice as Jack Gielgud? It's that drawing-room school of Shakespeare. Makes my blood boil. It has nothing to do with the violence, the passion, the *blood* of the Elizabethan stage. Did you hear my *Hamlet* on the radio?"

I had heard it on the *Columbia Workshop* last fall. God help me, but it was terrible. Even the papers had panned it.

(*Don't criticize.*)

"Yes," I said.

"What did you think?" He narrowed his eyes.

(Be hearty in your approbation and lavish in your praise.)

"Considering the time constraints you were under," I said, "trying to squeeze *Hamlet* into two half-hour broadcasts, I think the result was very close to brilliant."

I immediately regretted the *brilliant*—too transparently ass-kissing—Christ, my whole theatrical career wrecked with one astoundingly stupid word choice.

Welles pointed a black-gloved finger right in my face. "That is *exactly* correct. People criticized me for cutting 'To be or not to be,' but dramatically, in terms of pure story, that is the most expendable speech in the entire play."

"It doesn't tell us *one* thing we don't already know," I added.

"Can you sing?"

"I'm ready!" called the little man from the third-floor window.

"Plug it in!" yelled Welles. Then to me: "All right, Mr. Gielgud, sing me something. Astonish me."

My head was wild. This was my *audition*—on West 41st Street with the ambulance lights spinning and my hands rattling on drumsticks that were going to fly out of control at any second. This was Orson Welles leaning out his second-floor window, and a dozen ambitious, smart-ass actors watching, just hoping I'd mess up.

Sonja, the girl with the hairband, nodded at me in encouragement.

Gone, gone! Rodgers and Gershwin and "Have You Got Any Castles?" and "The Moon Got in My Eyes"—*gone!* I suddenly stopped playing the drums and sang out the only lyric on earth I could think of:

> *Won't you try Wheaties?*
> *They're whole wheat with all of the bran.*
> *Won't you try Wheaties?*
> *For wheat is the best food of man.*

"You're hired," Welles said.

My God. I hit the drumroll again.

"'Now let it work!'" yelled Welles to the upper-floor window. "'Mischief, thou art afoot. Take what course thou wilt!'"

And there was a sputter—a sizzle—

—and the single word M E R C U R Y blazed out hot red into the cold afternoon light.

People applauded and cheered.

A kid in a white restaurant apron with *Longchamps* stenciled on the pocket was running through the crowd carrying a silver-covered dish. "I've got the steaks for Mr. Welles!"

"I'm absolutely *starving* to death," said Welles. He took the silver tray and immediately handed it to the ambulance driver. "See if you can keep this warm." Then he lifted the lid of the tray to make sure everything was there. "Vakhtangov!" he shouted. "My pineapple juice!"

"Mr. Welles' pineapple juice!" called someone.

The pale skinny kid headed back into the theatre and tripped again on the doorjamb. "Rehearsal at 6:30, people!" Welles called. "And we're going to need everybody. John! This kid is going to play Lucius—the other son-of-a-bitch is fired."

"Orson, we absolutely need to commit to an opening date."

"Thursday! Thursday! I told you. We let Tallulah open on Wednesday in her three-million-dollar *Hindenburg* of *Antony and Cleopatra*. And then *we* open Thursday—a lean, brutal *Caesar*—a *Caesar* that will bestride the narrow world like a Colossus!" He slapped his hand on my back. "Sonja! Teach this kid the part. Know it by the time I come back, Junior, or you're fired. And to you, my mighty Mercury company, and to you, my mighty illuminated sign, how many ages hence shall this our lofty scene be acted over in states unborn and accents yet unknown! Behold, the Mercury Theatre!"

He bowed in mock grandeur, and the company broke into applause. Then he got into the front seat of the ambulance, the door was slammed shut, and, siren wailing, it took off down 41st Street.

Four

The official administrative offices of the Mercury were in the Empire Theatre Building (1430 Broadway), but its real center of activity was the tiny projection booth in the Mercury Theatre. Black metal stairs led up to this small airless room where, it seemed to me, one of the two telephones was always ringing. It felt like somebody's attic bedroom. There was an exposed boiling-hot radiator with the white paint peeling off. Two bookshelves were filled with scripts and mail; a small noisy icebox contained nothing but a carton of baking soda. Taped to the icebox door was a large black-and-white photograph of Orson Welles as Doctor Faustus, clutching his black robes to his neck, looking up into the smoky lights. Beneath it somebody had pasted a magazine ad for "Wilson's Tender Made Ham—The Ham You Cut with a Fork." There was one cast-off green armchair, heavily bandaged. Cardboard boxes on the floor were filled with stationery and envelopes that said THE MERCURY THEATRE in brown ink. There were two gray metal desks that looked like castoffs from the post office. There was a typewriter, an old table radio, an address finder, three bottles of Carter's ink, a

milk bottle blooming with some ancient roses, an
ashtray from the Stork Club, and dozens of 8x10
photographs on the floor, on the walls, pouring out of
the garbage can. Nailed and taped to the walls were
lobby cards and costume sketches from previous John
Houseman/Orson Welles productions. One depicted a
brown cartoon of a horse holding a hat in its mouth. It
read: *WPA Federal Theatre Project 891 presents Horse Eats
Hat—Maxine Elliot's Theatre 109 West 39th St.* On the
wall behind the refrigerator, thumbtacked into the
beaverboard, was a sinister-looking black poster of a
green smiling skeleton beating two green bones against a
tambourine hung around its waist. By its foot sat an
hourglass with sand running through it. Red letters
announced: *WPA Federal Theatre Project Presents Faustus
by Christopher Marlowe.* On the bulletin board above the
card table was tacked a calendar and the Mercury 1937-
38 subscribers list.

We were carrying up boxes of *Caesar* fliers, which
now joined the other boxes on the floor. There was a To
Do list on the wall, and Sonja crossed off "promo fliers."

"I'm Sonja—Sonja spelled with a J but pronounced
like a Y. Sonja Jones."

I sang to her the first line of "Have You Met Miss
Jones?"

"You're probably the hundredth person who's sung
me that."

"I bet I'm the cutest."

The phone was ringing. "Mercury," she answered brightly, moving to the typewriter and loading in a piece of paper with a pull of a ratcheted lever. "John's at 1430. Oh, then I don't know where he is. Yes, fine, I'll be absolutely sure to—" She typed with a jubilant violence, hung up the phone, tore the paper out of the machine, and tacked it to the wall under a label that simply read JOHN. Next to it was one reading ORSON. Next to that was OTHER. "Equity is on our backs for using unpaid extras," she said. She slid back the projection booth window. Below, onstage, men were hammering a series of gray platforms that filled the performing area. "And, listen—what's your name again?"

The phone was ringing.

"Richard Samuels."

She wrote it down. "Get it," she ordered. "Everybody's got to answer phones around here."

"Mercury!" I answered, and I thought to myself: *I'm the luckiest bastard on the face of the earth.*

"This is Brooks Atkinson from the *Times*," spoke the voice on the other end, "verifying a Thursday nine P.M. opening for *Caesar*."

The phone dropped heavily in my hands. "One minute, sir." I handed it gingerly to Sonja. "Brooks Atkinson," I whispered.

"Mr. A., this is Sonja. I got the roses; they were

absolutely beautiful. I've never seen that shade of yellow before. Yes, I'm sorry we keep changing the opening on you, but Thursday's firm." She crossed her fingers and gave me a goofy smile. "That means we won't change it for at least another hour. Yes, Armistice Day: it's Orson and John's little contribution to the war effort. Nine o'clock. Of course. And thank you once again for the roses. They made this whole place look cheerful."

The second phone was ringing, an older one with the mouthpiece mounted on the dialing column.

"Atkinson sends you flowers?"

"I did him a very small favor." She picked up the ringing phone. "Mercury Madhouse, I mean, Mercury Theatre." She giggled at her own joke. "This is she. Oh, Mr. Ingram, Orson left just two seconds ago...he took an ambulance to beat the traffic." She laughed. "Well, you know, according to Orson there's no law on the books that says you have to be *sick* to take an ambulance. Of course, that's according to Orson, which probably means it's not *really* true but that it *ought* to be." She checked her watch. "Yes, I know everybody's waiting, but I can assure you he'll be arriving any second—I know you made a special arrangement. I explained that to Orson. He understands the sacrifices you've made, and he's very grateful to you, believe me, we *all* are, and I'm sure he'll deliver a performance that's well worth the aggravation he's causing you. You know, whenever I listen to *The*

Shadow now I always think of you, Mr. Ingram? O.K. *Jerry*. And how wonderfully courteous you are to me. Most of the radio producers that call here are screaming and yelling. You're never like that. I think you're probably the most courteous and patient man I've met in the radio business." She rolled her eyes at me. "Thank *you* very much." She looked down at the floor and smiled. "I would be delighted to have lunch with you. This week we have the opening; it'll be hard. Yes, Orson's *Caesar* in modern dress—oh, absolutely brilliant—everybody marching around in military uniforms, brown shirts, Fascists—oh, absolutely the most astonishing thing you've ever seen.... Well, for anyone else it would be impossible, but for you Mr. Ingram, let me see what I can do." She was scribbling now. "Noon? The Onyx?"

Now the first phone was ringing again. "I don't know why the hell they don't call over to the Empire; John must have half a dozen people over there. Listen, let's take a runout powder. Orson wants you to learn the part by the time he comes back." She pulled a multigraphed script from the bookshelf and threw it to me. "Here ya go, Gielgud."

The four o'clock sunlight in Bryant Park lit the dust gold, and it burned in the windows on 42nd Street.

We split a hot chocolate as we sat on a bench and

filled in tiny black "11"s after the words "Opens November" on hundreds of *Caesar* fliers.

She laughed. "I'm making these elevens so bad nobody'll know *what* day we're opening. A Vassar scholarship and this is what I'm doing. If they ever found out how little work I'm doing in that college, they'd ship my ass back on the next train to Ohio." She stopped to look at the theatre pages in the *Times*.

"I never knew Ohio actually existed."

"Yahh," she said, and the falling cadence on the word was both comic and wistful. "Where they eat feesh on a deesh. I wish there were no rehearsal tonight. Barbirolli is conducting the *Pathetique* at Carnegie. Don't you absolutely love Tchaikovsky?"

"Adore him," I said.

"Usually I can get free tickets; I know this guy in Arthur Judson's office. This guy *pleaded* with me to go with him. So instead I'm filling in little elevens."

"I can learn the lines myself if you're attracted to pleading."

"No, I'm attracted to lying."

"Come again?"

"Sings? Plays the ukulele? I bet you can't even spell 'ukulele.'"

"Y-U—"

"'Taint funny, McGee."

"And how did *you* end up at the Mercury Theatre,

Miss-Sonja-with-a-J-but-pronounced-like-a-Y? By completely telling the truth?"

"I'm pleased to say I have *never* completely told the truth. John once told me that all of show business is based on bullshit, and the more I work here the more I think he's right. Anyway, I absolutely knew from the time I was ten that I *had* to get out of Ohio. I really did. Isn't it strange the way you *know* things as a child? As if there are currents pulling you. Orson told me he was directing plays when he was ten. I mean, how do you explain that? Sometimes I think the gods just know exactly what we're supposed to be doing, and they sit around patiently waiting for us to make the decisions we have to. You *can* play the ukulele, can't you?"

"You've heard of Ukulele Ike?"

"Sure."

"You don't know where I could find him, do you?" I said. "By the way, why does anybody play a ukulele in *Julius Caesar* anyway? Is Caesar singing 'Look for the Silver Lining' while they're stabbing him to death?"

"They've got it disguised as a lute. Lucius—that's you—sings Brutus a lullaby right before the final battle."

"I'm singing onstage?"

"You told Orson you could sing."

"Well, I can sing the Wheaties jingle. Who plays Brutus?"

"Orson."

Holy Jesus. I caught my breath, and I thought: Do I
really go with this—with this girl, this day, with what
was happening in front of my eyes? My head was sorting
through possibilities like some machine gone mad.
School? *Take the train in at night.* Matinées? Saturday was
no problem—so it was only Wednesday. *Get a waiver for
Wednesdays like those professional acting kids.* And how
was I supposed to get back for Caroline's show tonight?
And my part-time job at the Rialto?

Oh, I had some big-time lying ahead. But I also
knew—instantly, intuitively—that I was riding the
current of something enormous, important, possibly life-
altering. And a voice inside me said with perfect clarity:
Ride this, Richard. Ride this son-of-a-bitch as long as you
can. Lie your ass off; tell them *anything* but hang on. You
can always go back to Westfield High School. You can
always go back to mediocrity.

If you're scared for one second, Richard, it's all over.

I looked up at Sonja, at the sunlight falling on the
chestnut braid that held her hair.

I was in for the ride.

"Who was going to play Lucius before I showed up?"
I asked.

She shrugged. "Some kid. He had a personality
problem with Orson."

"Meaning?"

"Meaning he had a personality." She met my eyes.

"Look, Orson's very competitive, very self-centered, very brilliant. He's read everything. Knows everything. And the rule with Orson is you don't criticize him. Ever. So in the name of his talent, and in the hopes of working with him again, you forgive a lot of behavior that would be unforgivable among civilized people."

"And are you civilized people?"

"Are *you?*" she asked.

We were walking down 42nd Street toward Fifth. I was carrying the two heavy boxes of fliers.

"And you're doing all this for no money?" I said.

"For very little." She smiled. "I don't think you understand the power of celebrity, do you, Richard? Look, let's take two songwriters, all right?" She pointed to two men across the street. "They're both equally talented, they both write decent songs. But the first guy gets his song on the Hit Parade. And you see, he's suddenly *worth listening to*. The other guy may have exactly the same talent—maybe *more* talent—but for some completely ludicrous reason—bad timing, whatever—he doesn't get his song played. What I'm telling you is that the second guy is suddenly irrelevant. Doesn't count. You pass him on the street. *He makes no difference*. So why the hell am I working for nothing at the Mercury Theatre? Because I want something bigger than Vassar. I don't care if some teacher tells me I'm wonderful—some teacher who's never going to be

anything more than a teacher. I'm looking for something
so far beyond that. You know, I've got this girlfriend who
works for Ross at the *New Yorker*, the high-and-mighty
New Yorker—she tells me even there it's all running for
coffee and kissing his ass and laughing at his stupid,
vulgar jokes. I want something so much *bigger* than that.
And if the Mercury Theatre closes on Thursday night,
and it very well might, I know *twenty* people who would
fight to get me a job. Do you know who John promised
to introduce me to this week? David O. Selznick! This is
not bunk." Her voice was getting louder, and her eyes
were glowing. "David O. Selznick. The man who is
preparing to film *Gone with the Wind*. Do you have any
concept of the power of celebrity when you're dealing
with somebody on Selznick's level?"

"Does this mean you *won't* marry me?"

Five

I sat in a phone booth across from the New York Public Library, and I pulled the door closed. The seat was cold. There was a RE-ELECT LAGUARDIA sticker on the glass. *This is going to be hard.* I watched a few pigeons scatter along the curb, then I put the call through to my house.

"I have supper waiting," announced my mother.

"Mom, I'm in New York."

"Everybody's sitting down to eat. I made spaghetti with pot-cheese and cinnamon. Your favorite."

"Ma, I'm going to be stuck late in the city. There's an important research project I'm working on for school. I have to spend *hours* at the library; my whole grade depends on this."

Pause.

"And when are you coming home?"

"I don't know. Late. Late. So late I couldn't even— oh, Ma, here comes the librarian; save some spaghetti for me, all right? Gotta go. Love you!"

Sonja and I walked toward Times Square distributing

the fliers where we could: a shoe repair store, a
newspaper kiosk. I felt exhilarated and slightly out of
control—a good combination. I couldn't quite believe I
was walking next to this beautiful twenty-year-old girl
with her seamed stockings, her chestnut hair, and her
gently mocking eyes. Even strangers stared at her; guys
hurrying home from work slowed down—pushed their
hats back and looked over their shoulders to steal one
extra second's glimpse of her. I saw two guys shining
shoes; one of them eyed Sonja, tapped his friend on the
shoulder—*get a load of this*.

And I kept saying to myself: *why not?* I mean,
sometimes, Richard, you get lucky in this world, don't
you? Sometimes the wheel just lands on your number,
doesn't it? Who the hell was Orson Welles five years
ago? He was a seventeen-year-old kid. (*Every day, in
every way, my ego is getting bigger and bigger.*) Maybe if you
just wanted and believed something deeply enough, the
forces of the universe somehow conspired to make it
happen.

Yeah, and maybe they didn't.

What a night! What a girl! It was chop suey joints
and Arrow-collar guys and the smell of the subway
steaming up through the grates. It was the speakers in
the music stores playing "I'll String Along with You." It
was the illuminated letters of the *Times* news zipper
rolling out the headlines: CZECHS CONFIDENT   OF

WITHSTANDING GERMAN AGGRESSION. EXPECT NO ARMED
INVASION. It was the Astor Hotel and The Pause That
Refreshes and Gillette blades in blazing blue neon and
the huge illuminated bottle of Wilson's liquor ("That's
All") and Bond's clothing and Sunkist California
Oranges—Richer Juice, Finer Flavor—buzzing, blazing
scarlet, yellow, and white over every inch of Broadway.

It was one hundred voices at every streetcorner:

"That don't cut no ice with me, buster."

"Shuddup, ya lousy tart."

"What's the diff?"

It was kids on the corners hawking the *Herald
Tribune, Times, Daily News, Daily Mirror, Sun, Post,
Journal American, World Telegram.*...

Sonja and I stood in Nedick's eating hot dogs, the
wet rolls drenched in steaming sauerkraut. Between us
was the script for *Caesar.*

"You've got two real scenes," she said. "Both short."
She was flipping through the script. "Brutus—Orson—is
talking with Portia—Muriel Brassler—a bitch of the first
water, but nobody can say anything because Orson is
having an affair with her, right? Orson is married, you
know."

"Ah."

"Absolutely ah. Little Virginia. Very dark, very
pretty, very pregnant. They've got this tiny basement
apartment over on 14th, but he keeps her pretty much

locked away across the river at Sneden's. And if you ever hear somebody yell 'Anna Stafford!' that's code for Virginia; it means she's shown up unexpectedly and Orson better hide the ballerina he's trying to seduce."

"The Mercury is sounding more interesting all the time."

"And the *least* interesting part is *Caesar*. By the way, if anybody asks, you're an Equity Junior Member. And you're getting twenty-five dollars a week."

"Swell!"

"No, you're not *getting* twenty-five dollars a week. You're not getting anything, except the opportunity to get sprayed on by Orson's spit, but we've got enough Leftos in the company to start a demonstration if they find out you're not being paid. So first there's a knocking sound offstage. Portia exits. You enter." She pointed to my line in the script, and swallowed the last bit of hotdog. "You've studied acting?"

"You've heard of Eva Le Gallienne?" I said.

She nodded.

"You've heard of the Group Theatre?"

She nodded.

"Well, I never worked for either of them."

Six

Half an hour later I was sitting in an empty seat in the Mercury Theatre, and Norman Lloyd, who played the small role of Cinna the poet, was teaching me the chords to "Orpheus with His Lute," the song I was supposed to sing. I was trying to banter my way through the fact that I had no idea how to play the ukulele. Lloyd looked barely older than I was; he was the curly-haired guy I'd last seen trying to play the drums outside the theatre, and for some reason he seemed to get a kick out of me. He was sitting now on a theatre seat, his long legs bent painfully in front of him. Other actors milled around the stage—waiting. According to Lloyd, waiting for Orson was the principal occupation of the Mercury Theatre company. Lloyd was filled with an almost uncontrollable nervous energy; one of his legs bobbed continuously.

He strummed a terrible-sounding chord and sang:

Orpheus with his lute
Made trees and the mountaintops that freeze
Bend themselves when he did sing…

"What do you think?" he asked.

"I think you better hope Orpheus is deaf."

I turned around to see Sonja walking down the aisle balancing a coffee cup on a book.

Lloyd did an exaggerated double-take, and then played a stripper's bump-and-grind drumbeat on the back of the chair. He imitated a burlesque emcee: "I say, there goes another *big* one!"

"She and I had dinner tonight," I said.

"Yeah, right."

"I'm serious."

"You had dinner with the Ice Queen? Kid, every guy in this show's trying to get into her pants. Even Joe Cotten hasn't nailed her, and there's not a broad in the Manhattan phone book he hasn't—"

"Shhhh—"

She said, "Norman, could you verify that your bio is correct for the program? And initial it if it's O.K.?" Up close I could see she was reading *Gone with the Wind*. "Richard, I'll need your telephone number, too, if we need to reach you."

"She never asked for *my* telephone number," said Lloyd, not taking his eyes from the page proof. "How does this sound?" He read: "*Norman Lloyd started acting in vaudeville at the tender age of six and remained there for six years.* Does that sound like I remained at the age of six for six years?"

"If the shoe fits," said Sonja, and she got up to talk
to some other cast members.

Lloyd watched her. "Oh, sweet Jasper, I want to stick
my head under her sweater! I swear to you, I dream about
that sweater at night. I'd give ten bucks for just one good
photograph of her. I tell you, one good picture with a few
well-placed shadows would do wonders to ease my
nocturnal burden. Sonja! *Slake my urge!*" He hobbled
about between the seats, pretending to be bent double in
sexual frustration.

"She's your kind of girl?" I asked.

"If she said to me: 'Norman, I'll let you make love to
me, and I'll completely open myself up to you, and then
when we're done I'm going to shoot you in the head with
a pistol,' I'd say: 'Here's the pistol, baby—now let's get
started 'cause my hearse is double-parked.'"

The doors at the back of the theatre slammed open,
and Orson Welles entered carrying what appeared to be
two enormous phonograph records. There was a dark,
athletic-looking girl behind him. Then came some
technicians, followed by Houseman, whose English
accent was now sharpened with anger. "*How dare you,
Orson! We had discussed this.*"

"The Mercury Theatre will open when I say it's
ready to open," announced Welles.

"It's not as simple as that anymore, Orson. This isn't

the Federal. There *isn't* any front office. *We're* the front office."

A few feet from the stage, Welles turned on him icily. *"You're* the front office, Jacko. And you're starting to talk like a real bureaucrat, you know that? A small-minded, little copies-in-triplicate-and-please-God-don't-disturb-my-lunch-hour bureaucrat. I left the Federal to escape people like you."

"We left the Federal because they *fired* us, Orson. This is *our* show now. You can't go around forever playing Peck's Bad Boy and expect people will find it endearing. It isn't endearing, it's simply irresponsible."

"You started out as grain merchant; you'll always be a grain merchant."

"And your telling John Mason Brown that the opening date is still tentative is irresponsible, childish—"

"And accurate." Welles turned to two technicians who were carrying a large phonograph. "Set that up on stage."

"Orson," said Houseman, changing his tone. "I'm *pleading* with you. We have *subscribers*. We are trying to sell a season's worth of tickets to a repertory company, and you can't say to people who have made plans and arrangements, 'The play opens whenever I feel it does.'"

"The play opens when I'm convinced it's ready."

"Orson, the play opens Thursday. We cannot delay it again."

"This discussion is over."

"It isn't over. I don't care if you have to rehearse for five days straight, we're previewing Wednesday, and we're opening *Thursday*. If we delay this opening one more time, we're dead as a theatrical company."

"I cannot rehearse with this man in the theatre," announced Welles, clamping his hands over his ears. "Will someone tell me when he's left the building?"

Houseman headed halfway up the aisle, then turned. "This is an infinitely rewarding partnership, Orson. You go around *smashing* everything, disenfranchising every friend, every supporter we have. And then I'm left desperately trying to clean up your mess. I'm the one who ends up making the apologies, making the corrections—making the ten thousand phone calls I don't even *tell* you about."

"And I'm out acting in *The Shadow* and *The March of Time* and every other goddamn-son-of-a-bitch piece-of-shit radio show in this city, just to pour *my* money— my *personal* money, a *thousand* dollars a week, into this goddamn-son-of-a-bitch theatre that *you're* supposed to be running."

"That *I'm* supposed to be running!" said Houseman, the veins in his neck and forehead protruding. "Single-handedly, *I'm* supposed to be running the Mercury Theatre! I'm *killing* myself trying to run it! What in the hell are *you* doing for the Mercury Theatre?"

"I am the Mercury Theatre!" thundered Welles.

"I resign!" said Houseman. "You're on your own." He headed up the aisle.

"Just let me rehearse in peace!" said Welles with his arms stretched out to the heavens.

At this slightly conciliatory tone, Houseman stopped to listen.

"No director in the *history* of the theatre would work under conditions like these," declaimed Welles. "Sabotage. Jealousy. Every single member of this company deliberately attempting to destroy my work. But wait and see!" Welles had assumed a grandiose tone for the benefit of all of us. "I'll mount a *Caesar* that will astound the eye and the ear. It will be Shakespeare as it's not been seen since the time of Elizabeth herself— Shakespeare written in the language of tears and blood and beer—in the language of starlight and fireflies and the sun and moon! The only thing even near to it in the history of American theatre will be my own production of *Macbeth* last year. But this will be greater! Richer! Deeper!" He removed a rolled-up magazine from his jacket pocket. He was playing to the whole theatre now. "Did you see the cover of *Time?* Look at this. The goddamn-son-of-a-bitch *Lunts!* Well, let me tell you something—before this year is over I—*we*—will be on the cover of *Time.*" He gestured to the balconies. "This stage is where theatrical history is being written—with you and me and all of us as its principal players!"

"Orson—" began Houseman.

"Please! Let me rehearse in peace!" He held his ears again to stifle the imaginary clamor. "I will do the best I can for you. *Exhausted* as I am, I will attempt to rise above the arrogance and jealousy around me and get you your opening." He dramatically climbed the stepladder to the stage. "...the *small-mindedness* around here," he muttered to himself. "I'm *suffocating!*" Then he moved into a pool of light and gestured toward his female protégé. "Let it be said that here was a man who loved the Mercury not wisely but too well."

"Thursday!" said Houseman.

"Anna Stafford!" somebody yelled from the back of the house.

"Oh, Christ," said Welles, leaping from the stage.

Virginia Welles came walking down the aisle. She looked to be in her early twenties. She wore an oversized tweed coat, and you could see she was pregnant.

Meantime, Welles was hustling his female protégé into a seat in the fourth row. "You see, Betty, I believe it was Stanislavsky who said to Max Reinhardt—" He looked up, filled with surprise. "*Ginny!* What an unexpected and *delightful* surprise!"

Two steel fire doors opened from the alley onto the stage, and a dozen housepainters were led onstage by Sam Leve, the little man with the crewcut whom I had last seen installing the illuminated Mercury sign. Instantly, there were boxes of paint cans, splattered wooden ladders, rolls of dropcloths.

"Mr. Welles, what I had to do to find seventy gallons of red paint!" said Leve in his heavy Jewish accent. "But the paint is cheap; it's got a binder of fish glue in it, so don't blame me if it smells a little from fish. And I have something else to talk to you about."

"We also need to paint the platforms gray," said Welles. He gestured to the stage set, which consisted of three steps leading to a bare platform. From the backstage wall a ramp tilted up toward the main playing area. Four trap doors had been cut through the stage floor—two on each side—and smaller holes had been cut into the central playing area, each one covered with a strong wire grid. Below each grid was mounted a theatre light aiming directly up.

"*Mit en drinnen* I need gray paint? Mr. Welles, there's a saying in Jewish: *Mir kennet tanzen ahf svay chassenahs mit ain tuchis*. You can't dance at two weddings with the same rear end!" He removed a folded-up piece of paper from his pocket. "But I want to talk to you about the *Playbill*, the wording, the choice of words, there's a mistake here—"

Welles waved it off without looking at it. "I've corrected it already."

Leve pointed to a line. "It doesn't represent my

contribution."

"You're looking at the proof; it's all been corrected. See Sonja."

"Orson, we're ready to test this." The two technicians had by now installed the phonograph center stage.

"Coulouris!" shouted Welles, and his voice broke. "Vakhtangov, my pineapple juice!"

"Mr. Welles's pineapple juice!" someone shouted.

Vakhtangov ran toward the stage with a bottle of juice. He tripped, the bottle went flying. Lloyd leaped up, caught it—tossed it to Welles.

"Coulouris! Front and center!" Welles gulped down half the contents of the bottle in a single swig. "Where's that gloomy son-of-a-bitch? Vakhtangov! Find Coulouris and tell him to get his no-acting ass down here. Jesus Christ, who's directing this show!"

"That's what I'd like to know," said Lloyd to me quietly, but Welles had heard him. He pointed a threatening finger out to the audience. "One more comment like that, Mr. Lloyd, and your precious Cinna-the-poet scene hits the cutting-room floor."

"Are we ever going to actually *rehearse* my precious Cinna-the-poet scene, Orson?"

"Rehearse? I thought you were the great comic improviser, Lloyd. The Chaplin of the Federal! I see Cinna as a lofty, almost-Byronic figure. He's Shakespeare's indictment of the intelligentsia—his indictment of the ivory tower and—"

"I completely disagree," said Lloyd in a tone that was surprisingly tough. "He's a street poet without a cent for a cigarette. Unshaved. Poems sticking out of his shoes. The forgotten man. But the crowd's so crazy for blood they'll kill him anyway."

"Absurd interpretation," said Welles. "Completely unjustified by the text. A total violation of the spirit of the play, and *yet*, there may be *something* there I can use. *Coulouris!* Where is that—"

George Coulouris entered from stage left. He was a large man, and he wore a green military uniform with a black gun belt across the front. "I thought this was a dress rehearsal," he said, rubbing lotion into his hands. He disdainfully surveyed the clutter of the stage, the dozen housepainters rolling rust-colored paint on the entire back wall of the theatre. "Of course, the way you continue to cut the text, my character might as well not be in the play at all."

"Please! Antony's funeral oration is the dramatic centerpiece of *Caesar*," said Welles. "Every schoolboy in the world knows it. People in the audience will be whispering it with you."

"If they're still awake after those endless scenes between you and Gabel. Why every Cassius scene should be labored over—every precious, tedious exchange preserved—while the part of Marc Antony, a character universally acknowledged to be the *pivotal* role of the play, should be shorn down to forty lines is something I, of course, will never understand. But Gabel's the director's darling in this piece. Just as Olivier was when we studied together at Elsie Fogerty's Central School for Speech and Drama in London."

"We're going to record your speech," said Welles. "These two gentlemen are engineers from Mutual. Of course what's crucial to 'Friends, Romans, countrymen' is not so much the speech itself, but its effect on your audience." Welles was suddenly the professor. "You listen. You judge their reactions. You pause. You *tune* them to your ends."

Coulouris looked at him. "Do you imagine, Orson, you're telling me something I don't know?"

Then somebody was screaming. A painter, stepping back to look at his work, had fallen backwards through one of the open traps. Luckily, there was a mattress down in the cellar.

"That's it!" said Coulouris. "First, you cut my part to shreds; now you're trying to kill us all. I've never in my life been associated with such a ragtag production. Modern dress! We can't *afford* costumes. We can't even afford a stage that isn't gaping with holes."

"Stage traps are a tradition as old as Shakespeare," said Welles, "and I would have thought that even Elsie Fogerty's Central School for Speech and Drama in

London might have told you that stage traps comprise one of the most basic tools in the—"

"Let's go, Orson," said a technician.

Welles was suddenly pointing at me. "No kids in this scene. It's a vicious mob. I thought you were out somewhere, learning your lines."

"I know my lines," I said.

Welles fell instantly into his Brutus voice. "'Go to the gate. Somebody knocks.'"

"'Sir, 'tis your brother Cassius,'" I answered without hesitation. (I was beginning to learn the rules—whoever was the biggest son-of-a-bitch won.)

"'Is he alone?'"

"'No, sir, there are more with him.'"

"Not 'more' with him," said Welles. "'Moe' with him. This is Shakespearean verse we're speaking. Do you think you can arbitrarily change the words of the world's greatest playwright because you're not comfortable with them?"

"I meant—"

"Go home and learn your lines."

"I know them."

"And I say you need *moe* time. We're in one tiny scene, Junior, but remember that tiny scene serves to humanize the entire historical pageant of the play." Welles was back in the lecture room. "We cry for the death of Brutus because of that one scene. And that beautiful lullaby captures all his inexpressible sadness. A lullaby I interpolated, by the way, from *Henry VIII*, act three, scene one. Now go home and learn your lines. Have we given him the ukulele yet? Sonja! He needs the music for the song. Is there *anyone* here trying to—"

Welles screamed and disappeared down a hole in the stage.

I took the 10:07 Hudson Tube home to Newark, then transferred to the local. I sat in the near-empty car strumming my ukulele and softly singing, "Orpheus with his lute...." My ears were ringing with Shakespeare.

Caroline would have finished her performance in *Growing Pains* by now. The little towns passed in the night, the little lives. And here I was, riding this train with a multigraphed script for *Julius Caesar* on the seat next to me, practicing a song that Marc Blitzstein had written for my character—and on Thursday night I might be singing it before an audience of every significant theatre critic in New York City at the debut of the Mercury Theatre.

The voices sounded in my head over the clattering rails: Welles and Houseman and Lloyd and Coulouris and Sonja and Anna Stafford and Orpheus with his lute....

It was midnight, and I was as awake as I'd ever been in my life.

Sunday, November 7
Seven

It was probably around one in the morning when I got back to Westfield. I walked home from the train station, studying the shuttered, dreaming town: its porches, its nightlights, its wind and leaves and telephone wires. It seemed the quietest place in the world.

"I first met Orson Welles..." I began dictating to my interviewer.

A light had been left burning on the porch of my house, and from the street I could see a large garden rake left standing next to the door, a pair of work gloves next to it.

Even at one in the morning my domestic inadequacies spoke loudly.

The morning. The phone was ringing downstairs.
It was Caroline.
"I'm sorry I couldn't make it last night," I began.
"The show was canceled 'cause there was no heat in the building, so you didn't miss anything," she said.
Who understood the human heart? One day I was

ready to write off Caroline as a conspicuously wrong choice, and the next day I'd see her standing there in the sun in her pale yellow angora sweater and matching kneesocks, the light catching her hair, and I'd think: Richard, fall down on your knees and thank God this girl, of her own free will, is actually interested in you.

"And, listen, Richard, Mrs. Giaimo pulled me aside last night—and you can't tell *anybody* this, all right?"

"Who am I going to tell?"

"She said she's thinking about giving me the lead in the spring musical. I have to sing for her and everything; you know, go through all the motions, but she's *certain* it's going to be me—and, you know, Kristina Stakuna is *never* going to forgive me. But it's *so* exciting! I'm not supposed to tell anybody, but I had to tell you. I can't even think about it; it gets me too crazy. So are we getting together today?"

I suddenly knew I wasn't going to tell her about Orson Welles and the Mercury Theatre. Not yet. This was *her* moment—her lead in the spring play. And Orson Welles was still too fragile a dream: too impossibly wonderful, too perilous, and too achingly mine to tell anyone yet. When it was absolutely certain I was opening in the show, when it couldn't be canceled, when my part was perfect, and all I had to do was astonish them, then I'd tell them all.

"I think I'm going to be busy today," I said.

My mother walked into the kitchen. She spoke to me as if I weren't even on the phone. "Are you waiting for your father to pick up those leaves? Is that what you want? Sure, let the horse do it. All week long he works; he kills himself for this family. And you're on that phone day and night. *Sure, let the horse do it.*"

"Ma, I'm going to help; I'm on the phone right now."

"And he's out there now. Sunday morning. He's out raking leaves. With *his* back. And you—every two seconds you're running out that door."

"Ma! I'm raking right now. Caroline, I'll call you later!"

I raked the dead leaves into a pile in the backyard, and then began burning them in a wire metal trash basket. In about ten minutes the entire backyard was on fire, and my mother had to call the fire department.

"It's no use," she said.

At Newark I took the bus to Broad Street. I carried my ukulele and my script in a grocery bag. My clothes and skin still smelled like smoke.

I was working that fall for Leonard Goldberg, who managed the Rialto Theatre. He was fat and nervous; he chain-smoked Kools, and he was allergic to practically everything. He was also pretty much entirely incapable of dealing with other human beings, so he spent most of the day hiding in his office, sending me out for a "blueberry Danish and a Sanka-dark-half-sugar."

He generally let me run the place. First, I sold tickets at the window (that week it was *Broadway Melody of 1938*). Then, in between features, I'd walk center stage. "Good evening, ladies and gentlemen," I'd say, "and welcome to another gift night at the Rialto Theatre." Just this sentence usually got some applause. Then I'd reach into a wicker basket and draw out ten winning ticket stubs, reading the numbers out loud. The winners stood up, and I'd get the rest of the audience to applaud them. Later on, they'd come up to claim their broken lamps and their too-tight shoes or their year's supply of Fleischmann's yeast. What the audience didn't know— and what even Mr. Goldberg didn't know—was that I'd rigged the entire thing so that my family won every single drawing. Some nights it was my mother, other nights my grandmother, my sister, my Aunt Minnie. When I'd sell them their tickets, I'd write their ticket numbers on the palm of my hand. Then, onstage, I'd reach into the basket, pull out a ticket, then read the number on my palm. "And the first of tonight's lucky winners is number 0144!" My Aunt Minnie would cry out in surprise. Or my grandmother would stand up smiling. My sister was the best at winning; she'd scream, jump up and down, hug her girlfriend.

Pretty soon all our houses were filled with enough

boxes of dishes and glassware to entertain twelve thousand for lunch.

I told Mr. Goldberg that I wouldn't be able to work that evening's show, or any night that week, because of a "death in the family."

"*Ah bruch*," he said. "Who died?" He sneezed messily into his handkerchief.

"My Aunt Minnie."

His hands were shaking as he tried to light a Kool. "The whole week you're gonna need?" he asked. Then he cleared his throat and spat into his handkerchief.

"We have to sit shiva."

"Naturally. Naturally. But *(sneeze)* I'll tell you something, Richie, it kind of leaves me in the lurch, doesn't it?"

"If you like, Mr. Goldberg, I can get my friend Phil Stefan to do it; he's completely square, and he'd be glad to pick up the extra jack."

"Could you do that for me, Richie? *(Volcanic sneeze)* Oh, Jesus, that one got all over you, didn't it?"

More madness. Another train, and I made it downtown by one o'clock. Welles had told me to be at the theatre by noon. I ran all the way to the Mercury— steering northeast with every green light; horns honking; people yelling.

I came whipping down 41st Street, and I pulled back the metal gate of the stage door, entering where the insiders did.

The theatre smelled like rotten fish. People were waving away the noxious fumes, and two large electric fans were aimed at the back theatre wall in an effort to dry the horrible-smelling paint.

But it *looked* terrific—the entire back brick wall was painted blood red.

Muriel Brassler, the dark-haired beauty who played Portia, was complaining to Welles about the lights. "These are all wrong for me, Orson. I *cannot* work with these."

"They look fine," said Welles, who was trying to block his scene with her and work out the lighting cues at the same time.

"Orson, I never heard of lights with no color in them. Where are the gels?" She was dressed in her pale blue gown; Welles wore his black military overcoat.

"Muriel, let's worry about the gels later," he said.

She picked up a large manila envelope. "Barrymore Pink is the only color that effectively highlights the natural tonalities of my skin." Then she removed from the envelope some plates of colored glass. "Believe me, I know what works for me."

Welles stared at her in disbelief. "She packs her own

gels."

"I have *one* scene, Orson. Allow me my one scene? Jeannie! Please put these in, dear?"

The lighting assistant came out from the wings.

"Do whatever she says," said Welles hopelessly. "I just don't want to hear any more about tonalities. Can we at least *block* this scene? Can we make *some* progress here? All right, I'm reading the letter downstage right." He assumed his slightly professorial Brutus voice. "'But 'tis a common proof that lowliness is young ambition's ladder, whereto the climber upwards turns his face. But when he once attains the upmost round—'"

"Is that where you're going to be standing?" asked Muriel. Her hand was on her hip.

"Yes, my dear. Would you like to redirect the play? Maybe we can bathe the entire audience in Barrymore Pink."

"I have a two-page scene, Orson. Two effing pages."

"What, in the *depths* of your ignorance, do you want me to do?"

"I am simply worried that the difference in our height—"

"Your height! I swear to God, Muriel, if you mention your height to me one more time I'm cutting this scene. Your height is fine! Nobody thinks you're too tall except you."

"I look like some kind of effing giant next to you!

People are going to laugh."

"Nobody is going to laugh. Nobody is even going to be looking at you."

"There, you see! Nobody's going to be looking at me!"

"You are deeply disturbed. Look. Nobody is going to be looking at you because they'll be *listening* to you—transported by the poetry. *That's* the magic of this play, not the goddamn-son-of-a-bitch Barrymore—"

"All I want," she said with her hand to her chest, "and I do *not* think this is unreasonable, is for you to take one step up the ramp before I enter."

"Anything you say, Muriel."

Muriel looked up toward the lighting assistant, who was standing on a ladder now. "Can you aim that spot directly down, dear? When the light hits my face correctly, a tiny butterfly-shaped shadow appears under my nose. That's when you know you've got it right."

The fire doors on the side of the stage opened, and Houseman led onstage a gigantic Negro man dressed in African tribal costume; he was holding a long staff with a screaming animal skull at the end of it.

"Meestah Whales! Meestah Whales!"

"Abdul!" cried Orson, and he hugged the tribal chieftain.

"Abdul need five teek! Opening night." He shook his staff.

"Abdul did the drumming for my Haitian *Macbeth*," explained Welles to the company.

"Abdul need five teek for *Caesar!* Opening night!"

"I don't know if—"

"If I no get, bad spirit in theatre! Bad review!"

Orson went pale. "John, give him the tickets. That's all we need now: the Bad Luck Thing."

Welles rehearsed the funeral oration scene until everybody was sick of it. Now he had the actors stomping the platforms as they demanded to hear Caesar's legacy. ("The will! The will!")

Joe Cotten, Norman Lloyd, and I sat in the audience and watched Welles yelling out the light cues.

I had unerringly been drawn to the two least serious members of the company. The major source of our entertainment was Cotten's inexhaustible tales of his sexual conquests. Cotten really was an astonishingly handsome young man, with a leading man's curling blond hair and blue eyes. Lloyd had nicknamed him "Fertilizer."

Cotten was sitting in the seventh row with Lloyd and me cataloguing all the New York theatre women he had slept with during the past two months. He was counting on his fingers, and he'd moved onto his second hand. "There was Jeanette Bradley. She and I got together the night after she broke up with Orson. I broke up with her twice, each time for two days, and during those two days I messed around with Jeanette Lee, Velma Lord, and Kate Fredric, who asked me if I would go to bed with her and her twin sister, but I told her no. That was too much even for me."

"Fertilizer draws the moral line," said Lloyd.

"Then I got back together with Jeanette Bradley, but she dicked me over by sleeping with Orson again. So that same night I met up with both Evelyn Allen and Muriel Brassler."

"What's the dope on Muriel?" Lloyd asked, looking at the stage. "I heard she's a gymnast."

"She's got a gymnast's body, I can tell you that."

"Did she get a firm grip on your monkey bar?"

"Tell me about Evelyn," I said. Evelyn Allen played Caesar's wife. Her part only ran about a page and a half, but you stopped to notice her. She had these lovely arms, bare to the shoulder. Backstage, she always sat by herself reading a book. "I think she's got style."

Lloyd and Cotten leaped into some old vaudeville schtick of theirs:

"I like her *style*."
"I like her *smile*."
"I like her *class*."
"I like her—*other features*."

They found this extremely amusing, and, once again, Lloyd played his stripper's bump-and-grind drumbeat on the seat as he sang out: "Oh! Doc! I-feel-so-good! Meetcha-round-the-corner-in-a-half'n-hour!"

"I'm kind of fascinated by her," I said. "I always wonder what she's reading. She's got class."

"She's gotta big *what?*" said Cotten.

"A toast to class!" said Lloyd. He lifted his bottle of root beer, and intoned: "The deep red wine may *kiss* the glass; and *you*, my friend—"

"Farewell forever," finished Cotten.

"What *is* she reading?" I asked.

"This kid's got the hots for every broad in the show!" said Lloyd. "Who the hell cares what she's reading. It's those bee-stung lips! God, I want to bite those bee-stung lips." He gestured to the back of the theatre, where Sonja had entered eating a tangerine. "Now here's a cute little lass."

"Nice face, too," said Cotten.

I had tried not to think about her all morning. I had said to myself: All right, Richard, this girl is older than you. You think she's beautiful, but *everybody* thinks she's beautiful. *She* thinks she's beautiful. Time to grow up, Richard. You want to be taken seriously, then look at reality. Girls aren't knocked out by you. They *like* you. They're charmed by your courtesy, your boyishness. They don't look at you in any sexual or romantic way.

You're kind of sweet, amusing, but their hearts don't drop, *oh, God*, when you enter the room. This girl's made it from Nowhere, Ohio, to the Mercury Theatre on nerve and beauty and ambition. Get a hold of your monkey bar, Richard.

God, I hated being the nice guy. Skelly and Stefan got every girl in the school. I mean, they actually were allowed to *touch* them. But Skelly and Stefan were athletes. Stars. They were the "Fertilizers" of Westfield High School.

And I played the drums at the football games and watched the girls in the stands; watched the beautiful, unapproachable girls like Kristina Stakuna joke with each other in their made-up Spanish slang. And their scarlet lipstick. I watched Kristina walk to the hotdog stand every five minutes just to talk, and she stood with her back to the game and smoothed her hair and pulled down the edges of her oversized sweater.

Sonja walked right up to me. "Hey, Richard. How's my favorite Equity Junior Member?"

"Is that a new blouse?" Cotten asked. "I don't think I've seen that one before."

"Actually, it *is* new," she said. "Thank you for noticing." She was wearing a blue long-sleeved shirt and blue jeans.

Cotten gestured to her copy of *Gone with the Wind*. "Still reading my favorite novel?"

She finished her slice of tangerine and licked her fingers. "I'm annotating it so when I meet with Selznick we'll have something specific to talk about."

Lloyd said, "And when, may I ask, are you meeting Selznick?"

"John's trying to get him here for opening night."

"Are you kidding?" said Lloyd. "I'm going on in a completely unrehearsed scene—and David O. Selznick is gonna be here? Oh, sweet Jasper, I'll end my Broadway career and my Hollywood career at the same time. Thrift! Thrift!"

"That'd be quite a coup if you could actually meet him," said Cotten.

"Oh, I'll meet him," said Sonja.

"Tell him I'm available for Ashley."

"Actually you have the right face for Ashley."

"You know, Sonja," said Cotten, seamlessly, "there's this *exquisite* little place I discovered in the Village—you loved Amalfi when I took you there? Well, you're going to love this place; called Marta, down on Waverly. Would you let me take you there tonight after the rehearsal? It's open late."

Pounce, I thought.

"It's a wonderfully generous offer," she said, "but I've got a date with Richard."

She touched me lightly on the arm, smiled, and headed toward the stage.

The two gentlemen turned to me in stunned disbelief.

"She's kidding! She's kidding!" I said.

"Oh, Fertilizer, you better turn in your seed bag," said Lloyd. "This kid's heading for some seafood-momma."

"Last exit before quadruple-space," said Cotten.

"Before what?" I asked.

He explained: "You know—when you read a novel, and the main characters are finally about to *shtup*? Well, they can't *describe* anything or they couldn't print the book. They just go, 'He hugged her hard, and they fell into bed.' Period. *Quadruple space*. Next paragraph the sun is rising and the milkman is knocking the bottles together. All the good stuff happened in the *quadruple space*."

"Fertilizer's hoping to make his next thirty years one long quadruple space," said Lloyd.

"Have you ever...with...?" I asked.

"Goddamnit, I tried," said Cotten. "Dinner, dancing...I must have spent thirty dollars on that broad."

"Still no quadruple-space?" I asked.

"I still haven't heard the milkman knocking the bottles together."

"A bet," said Lloyd. "Two bucks to the first guy who gets into Sonja's pants."

"That is unspeakably crude," said Cotten.

"It's cheap and demeaning," I added.

We sat for a moment in silence.

"O.K....*five* bucks," said Lloyd.

Eight

A t eight that night we ran through the first real dress rehearsal of *Caesar*—music, lights, military uniforms.

I stood on a mattress under the upstage trap, in the basement really, waiting for my cue. Behind me stood Grover Burgess, dressed as Ligarius, in a torn scarf and oil-stained raincoat.

Up above me the conspirators were whispering. The entire rehearsal so far had been a disaster, and Welles kept breaking character to scream about everyone's incompetence.

"'Our course will seem too bloody, Caius Cassius,'" said Welles "'to cut the head off and then,' *Jesus Christ*, Jeannie, I told you to turn off everything but the goddamn work light. *How many times—*"

I stood there with one foot resting on the stepladder. The smell of the paint was still heavy. Someone's step creaked on the platform overhead. My leg was shaking uncontrollably.

"'But it is doubtful yet whether Caesar will come forth today....'"

"'Never fear that.'"

"'By the eight hour. Is that the—'"

My cue.

"Break a leg," said Burgess.

"With this ladder, I probably will." As I headed up toward the conspirators, I imagined what my rising head must look like to an audience. I could hear Burgess ascending right behind me.

The platform creaked under my step. *One line, that's all this is—*

I said aloud: "'Here is a sick man that would speak to you.'"

"Louder!" said Welles.

"'Here is a sick man that would speak to you.'"

"Good. Now exit left."

I walked into the wings where the four-man orchestra sat watching.

"How'd I do?" I asked.

The drummer looked up from his men's magazine. "What?"

Caesar had no intermission, and I silently moved to the back of the house to watch some of the big scenes— Coulouris on the black velvet-covered pulpit screaming for silence: *Friends, Romans, countrymen! Lend me your ears!* Below him the thirteen lights cut into the stage floor shot directly upwards. It looked like the *Life* magazine pictures of the Nürnberg rallies.

Sonja sat near me at the back of the house. She tucked her blue-jeaned leg under her. Even in work clothes there was something a little provocative in her presence—her chestnut hair smelled like black licorice. She sneezed, and she whispered, "I've got the Mercury cold. Don't get too close to me. Read this."

She handed me a typewritten piece of paper.

Selznick International
230 Park Avenue
New York City

Sonja Jones: John Houseman speaks in glowing terms of your talents and tells me you've got some first-rate ideas for our "Civil War picture." We'd love to hear them. DOS in town this week. Please give us a call as soon as it's convenient.

> *Sincerely,*
> *Katharine Brown, Story Editor*

"Wow."

"This is one of those letters that change your life, Richard. Four sentences and everything in your future is altered."

For a moment she watched the scene being rehearsed onstage. "I hate actors; I really do. They've got that invisible camera following them around everywhere they go. *Hey, folks, did you see the way I walked up that ramp? Did you see the way I tilted my hat?* They make me ill. They really do."

"If you hate actors, why are you hanging around with me?"

"You're not an actor. You just haven't figured it out yet."

"Is that an insult?"

"It's the opposite of an insult."

"Well, you don't like actors. What kind of guys *do* you like?" I asked and I thought, Here we go again, Richard. The buddy. The best friend. Sonja was talking, and I was remembering last summer. Stefan's girlfriend, Kate Rouilliard, had called me up at midnight—crying. I'd met her in the bleachers across from the high school.

"I can't understand why he *turns* on me," she said wiping her eyes. "It would be different if I hurt him or something, but I haven't done anything. He just turns so *cold* on me. I don't understand guys, Richard. I really don't."

I sat there holding her hand, trying to console her, trying to disguise my sideways erection. Her face was wet and perfumed, and I stared at her bare ankle in the moonlight.

"Richard, I don't know what I'd do without you. You're the best friend I've got. I'm sorry to always be *drowning* you in this emotional crap." She got up from the bleachers. "I wish there was something I could do for you."

Just unbutton your shirt, Kate. Just leave it unbuttoned for thirty seconds.

"I always thought being a beautiful woman would be terrifically interesting," I said to Sonja. I was trying to widen the scope of the conversation, and I thought the *beautiful* might get her attention. It was code for: I'm in love with you like everybody else, but I'm much too suave to say it. "To watch the world sort of fall at your feet whenever you show up. To know what that feels like. Does this mean I'm a homosexual?"

"Yes. Mostly I despise the way I look. My neck is too long. My eyelids have too much skin on them."

"Your eyelids! Sonja, you're nuts."

"Really, I'm one huge catalogue of faults."

"Name me one fault."

She thought a second.

"My left breast is smaller than my right."

"Have you got a ruler?"

Onstage, Marc Antony had finished shouting about the generosity of Caesar's will ("To every man—seventy-five drachmas!") and the mob had dispersed, their thick-soled shoes drumming the platforms.

Lloyd, as Cinna the poet, entered right. He was looking rumpled and bewildered. Some citizens entered left.

"'I dreamt tonight,'" he began, "'that I did feast with
Caesar...I have no will to wander forth of doors. Yet
something leads me forth.'"

The citizens began questioning him:

"'What is your name?'"

"'Whither are you going?'"

"*Stop!*" yelled Welles. "Stop! This is *worse* than
terrible. You're lucky there's no intermission in this play,
Lloyd; they'd come back with rotten fruit. People, let's
come back to this scene later. We're pushing the river."

"The scene's not working because you never let us
rehearse it," said Lloyd.

"I'm thinking out loud," said Welles, now standing
in the orchestra. "If we cut this scene and moved directly
to the tent scene...you know, make it a blackout and a
musical interlude—just time passing—we might get
away with—"

"This scene is more than about time passing, Orson,"
insisted Lloyd from the stage. "It's about what happens in
a mob."

"Why don't we give Cinna a monocle," said Welles.
"You're playing him too working class."

"He *is* working class."

"I see a monocle, a long coat. Maybe a top hat. This
could be a laugh scene."

"Orson, the correct reading for this scene is the one

I'm giving it."

"Then convince me," said Welles, lighting a cigar. "Because right now it's dead." He folded his arms in front of him. "Go on, Mr. Lloyd. *Astonish me.*"

The entire company (except Welles, Houseman, and Sonja) headed toward a cafeteria on Broadway. In our olive-green uniforms, we looked like some disreputable unit of Army deserters.

Up ahead, leading the pack, were Joe Holland and George Coulouris, both loudly maligning Martin Gabel. Next were the two ladies: Muriel and Evelyn. Muriel checked her reflection in every shop window we passed. Evelyn carried her book.

At ten P.M. on a Sunday night the cafeteria was jumping. A spilled tray of coffee cups crashed to the floor; the theatre crowd applauded.

Outside, the headlights streamed down Broadway.

Inside, we were loud and obnoxious and generally in love with ourselves.

"What show are you people with?" asked a guy at the table next to ours.

"The *Jewish Julius Caesar*," said Lloyd. "Oy, Caesar, you shouldn't *know* from I saw in the sky tonight. Comets, thunder—oy, such a *headache* I got."

"Who are you?" asked Cotten.

"I'm Cinna! Cinna the *farkaktah* poet!"

"From this, Cinna, you make a living?"

"Give'm a glass tea."

"Tyranny is dead! And I get *such* a pain when I bend."

We ran through the second half of the play more quickly. The lighting cues were more effective now—swift, shadowy, fluid as a film.

"'*Lucius!*'"

Gabel was exiting the upstage ramp as I stepped out from the wings.

"'Lucius!'"

"'Here my good lord.'"

"'What, thou speak'st drowsily? Poor knave, I blame thee not. Thou art o'er-watched. Look, Lucius, here's the book I sought for so.'"

Welles had wandered down to the apron of the thrust stage—only a few feet from the audience. I followed him there. The lights were dimming slightly. Welles, in his military coat and leather gloves, sat on the small step that led to the main playing area. He pretended to read his small book.

He gestured that I also sit—and I did, next to him.

I was sitting on the empty stage of a Broadway house. We were too cheap to run the heat with no audience, and the place was freezing. I could smell the fresh gray paint of the platforms. There was no one under those

lights but me and Orson Welles—and floating between
us were words written four hundred years earlier. I was
trying to keep the nervousness out of my voice. *Don't lose
your place, Richard. What are the chords to the song? You
should have practiced it more.*

Welles said, "'Canst thou hold up thy heavy eyes a
whiles and touch thy instrument a strain or two?'"

"'Ay, my lord, an't please you.'"

"Slower," said Welles.

I nodded and thought: *Please, God, just let me
remember the goddamn song.*

"'I trouble thee too much, but thou art willing,'" said
Welles tenderly.

"'It is my duty, sir.'"

What was the second chorus?

"'I should not urge thy duty past thy might. I know
young bloods look for a time of rest.'"

"'I have slept, my lord, already.'"

B-flat to what? C or F?

"'It was well done, and thou shalt sleep again. I will
not hold thee long.'"

Thursday every theatre critic in New York would be
sitting there—every seat in the second balcony filled.

My right hand strummed an F, but since the
musicians had retuned the ukulele it sounded too high.

I sang in a reedy, nervous tenor:

Orpheus with his lute
Made trees and the mountaintops that freeze
Bow themselves when he did sing...

The lights were dimming completely now—nightfall, moonlight. *Fade the damn lights already.* The horns and drums picked up the melody.

In the dark Welles gave my shoulder a light touch. "Needs work, Junior."

Monday, November 8
Nine

My alarm clock went off at 6:55. I turned up the thermostat downstairs and added more water to the boiler.

I did my exercises on the bedroom floor: sit-ups and push-ups. "Every day in every way I'm getting better and better—*one!*"

That morning the radio was playing "I Can't Get Started with You."

"'I'm a glum one,'" I sang along with the verse. "'It's explainable....'"

Sara was up now; I could hear the shower running. Because she usually left the door open a quarter of an inch to vent the steam I could sometimes catch a glimpse of her standing naked in front of the mirror. It was sort of a sleazy thing to do, but I was feeling the increasing necessity of seeing a girl naked. And my standards were getting lower every day.

I ate the same breakfast every single morning: Fig Newtons and coffee (*"Hearty and nutritious," he said, spitting out all his teeth.*) And this particular Monday I sat with my legs jammed against the kitchen radiator, determined to feel the first stirrings of warmth.

"Mommy's going to kill you," said Sara, bopping into the kitchen, already dressed, scented, and perfectly groomed.

"For what?"

"*For what?*" She whittled down a couple of carrots and then ate them aggressively. "For coming in after midnight on a school night."

"Hey, I was helping Caroline and the play people strike the set, and we—"

"Strike the set, huh? And why would they be striking the set when the play was *canceled?* You better get your story straight, twerp." She bit into another carrot, enjoying her power. "And I've got something else you better get your story straight on."

I fanned the air. "Why do you wear so much of that stuff?"

She ignored me and pulled her chair closer. "You know your little girlfriend, Caroline?"

"She's not my girlfriend; she's my friend."

"She certainly isn't your girlfriend. Joan was at that party Saturday night over at Kristina Stakuna's house, and Joan told me she saw your little friend Caroline dancing her sweet little behind off with your big buddy Phil Stefan! Everybody in the whole school knows about it."

"You think I care?" I said, and I threw my plates noisily in the sink. "Jeez, the *small-mindedness* of people around here."

"I *told* you she was just hanging around you to get near him."

I held my hands to my ears. "I am *suffocating!*"

Of course Stefan's pursuing Caroline was exactly what you'd expect from the lying, drunken, horny, overly developed son-of-a-bitch. He couldn't wait *five* minutes to pounce?

I slammed the door and headed toward school.

The morning sky was perfect blue. Tangerine-colored leaves filled the steps and the sidewalks and the gutters and the flowerbeds. The trees looked like enormous sculptures, vaulted up into the sunlight, creaking. A man stood on a ladder putting up storm windows, and the morning smelled of rain and woolen scarves.

First class was Shakespeare with Dr. Mewling. He was in his early sixties, and he conducted every class in exactly the same manner: he took attendance, sat behind his desk, and then read us his notes for one hour straight. They were written on yellow legal sheets—God only knew how old they were—and he carefully returned each page to the bottom of the stack, perfectly prepared for next year's lesson. "Now, ladies and gentlemen, the woman Shakespeare married was *clearly* already with child when he *married* her, and her name was? Her name

was? Don't overwhelm me now. No one remembers?"
And here he didn't even bother to look up to see if
anyone might *attempt* to remember. He just kept talking.
"Well, let me tell you. Anne Hathaway." He'd glance at
the wristwatch he kept on his desk to keep us from
noticing that he was checking the time every two
minutes. "Now, ladies and gentlemen, the Earl of
Southampton was Shakespeare's patron. Do we know
what a patron is? A patron?" His eyes never left his
notes. "Don't everybody speak at once now. Well, ladies
and gentlemen, let me tell you. A *patron*—"

It was beyond ghastly. It was a sort of deranged
monologue in which the presence of the students was
entirely irrelevant. If anyone in that room had ever held
the remotest affection for Shakespeare it was being bled
from us, page by yellowed page—*any questions, don't
overwhelm me now.*

The only thing at all interesting about that
morning's one-hour prison sentence was that Kristina
Stakuna was late. Of course, the Amazon Queen of the
Swollen Softballs was always late; she'd sweet-ass it into
class ten minutes after the bell sounded, wagging her
little rich-girl's note on pink stationery. And Mewling
would read it, smile, and gesture to her to take her usual
seat. The Black Crow Crew had this joke that all her
notes read: *To Whom It May Concern: Please excuse
Kristina's lateness this morning, but her breasts are so*

enormous that she finds it difficult to walk at a normal speed.

That morning the student teacher was sitting in Kristina's usual seat, and the only other empty chair (besides the one directly in front of Mewling) was right next to mine. There was simply no way she couldn't sit next to me. My heart accelerated just thinking about it. I could see it all: she'd come in late with her gray sweater with the blue *W* sewn across the front. She'd stand there looking confused for one adorably sweet second—then she'd sit down next to me.

I was ready. *Rule Number Two: Smile.* Kristina, I heard the play was canceled. You must be *so* disappointed. You know, I was wondering, could I come over some night for extra help on my Spanish? Why don't we work up in your bedroom—it's so damn noisy in this kitchen? Tell me, Kristina, a few of us were wondering if it was really true that your boyfriend screwed you for nine hours?

Mewling lectured on; months passed; seasons changed. "Now, Shakespeare dedicated his first poem *Venus and Adonis* to whom? Don't all jump in here at once. To the Earl of *Southampton*, now isn't that a coincidence, ladies and gentleman. Shall we move on? *(places page on bottom of pile, realigns stack, glances at watch)* Part Two—The Histories: A Period of Development—1594-1600. Please make sure this is in your notes, ladies and gentlemen, hint, hint."

The door opened—loudly, boldly—and there was Kristina Stakuna, in her seventeen-going-on-twenty-seven magnificence. *Gentile angels walk the earth*, I thought. And some poem began taking shape in my head: *O, women of Westfield!* Gray sweater with a blue letter *W*. She handed Mewling her pink note. She took in the room in one glance—oh, the beautiful consternation of her lightly freckled face! And there was smiling Richard—and there was that barbarically empty torture-chair directly in front of Mewling.

She sat directly in front of Mewling. *I couldn't believe it*. She had never sat in the front row of any classroom, ever, in any class, in eleven years.

I watched as she opened up her purple notebook and began writing in her enormous, looping script.

I looked at the empty seat next to me. It was as if she couldn't even *see* me, as if her eyes couldn't even register my impression.

I sighed, and I shut my eyes.

"Mr. Samuels?" called out Dr. Mewling.

I opened my eyes. It was pick-on-the-idiot-who-hasn't-been-listening-and-humiliate-him-in-front-of-the-class time. The whole class turned to look at me (except, of course, for Kristina).

"You don't seem to be taking any notes today? You *know* all this material already, Mr. Samuels? Because if you do then perhaps *you'd* like to teach the class—you're apparently so knowledgeable about the historical plays of William Shakespeare?"

I looked up to challenge his gaze. He stared back at me with all the passion of a three-month-old corpse.

Mistake.

"Mr. Samuels seems to have his *mind* on other things this morning, ladies and gentlemen. We were discussing Shakespeare's histories. Perhaps you'd care to offer us *your* thoughts on the histories, Mr. Samuels; you appear to find the taking of notes so *completely* superfluous?"

Silence.

I spoke as loudly as I could. "I believe the greatest of Shakespeare's histories must be *Julius Caesar*."

"*That's* what you believe."

"And I know we're not starting it until next week, but I read it over the weekend for my own edification. Take, for instance, the brief but telling scene between Brutus—'the noblest Roman of them all'—and his serving boy, Lucius. That tiny, almost insignificant scene serves to humanize the entire historical pageant of the play. And that beautiful lullaby Lucius sings. Interpolated, I believe, in most productions from *Henry VIII*, act three, scene one."

The bell rang.

"See me after class," said Mewling.

* * *

Later that morning I sat in the back of Spanish class with Stefan. Señora Katz had spent the last twenty minutes trying to get the slide projector to work. She'd spent the first twenty minutes trying to get the screen to stand up.

"I heard you put the moves on Caroline, Judas," I said to Stefan.

"I danced with her, all right? She *begged* me to. If I hear about this one more time—"

"I thought you're seeing Kate Rouilliard."

"I *am*, but Caroline kept grabbing my ass all night, all right?"

"Drift, you can have any woman you want. You have to mess around with Caroline?"

"I'm not messing around with her, all right? The Black Crow is loyal to its own."

The slide projector finally came alive. The slides were illustrations from *Los de abajo*, the novel we were supposed to be reading. Señora Katz read us the caption: *"¡Qué hermosa es la Revolutión, aun en su misma barbarie!* Can anybody translate that?"

There was this girl sitting across the room from us who was wearing a loose-fitting dress, and she sat with one leg bent upwards and the other stretched out so that you could see all the way up her long legs to her black underwear. She raised her hand. *"How beautiful is the revolution even in its very barbarism.*"

Stefan nudged me. "*¡Qué hairmosa!*"

I was out roaming the halls with my bowling pin lavatory pass when I met Kate Rouilliard coming out of the first-floor bathroom. She raised her hand in protest before I could speak. "I heard already."

"It was just one dance."

"That he could do this to *both* of us is just so typical," she said. She leaned against a locker. No socks. "You once told me I was too good for him. I should've listened to you."

I laughed. "Maybe we'd both be better off if we started dating each other."

"I wish I weren't so supersensitive about him."

She looked right through me. *The Invisible Man Returns.* I willed her to say: *Why am I hanging around with him anyway, Richard? It's right in front of our eyes, isn't it? Right in front of our eyes, and how come we've never seen it before? How could we be so goddamned blind? You're the one I talk to; you're the one who's been my best friend—*

"Do you think he loves me, Richard?"

"I'm certain of it, Kate."

"You're one of the very few people I trust not to lie to me."

"Listen, Kate, could you do me a favor?" *Unbutton your shirt.*

"Oh, dear. Sometimes I think the only reason people are friendly to me is because I work in the attendance office."

"I have to get out of here by noon. You've got to get my name on the absence list."

"I can get your name on the list, but if they call home to check, you're screwed."

"They're not going to call home for me. I've never cut once. I have credit in my account. Will you do it?"

Ten

Even the New Jersey swamps seemed worth studying that afternoon as my train clanked along toward New York. Has there ever been a more delicious feeling than being suddenly set free from school?

¡Qué hermosa!

The morning sang in possibilities: all the time in the world! And my vision suddenly felt sharper, richer, unoccluded.

I sat on a bench in Bryant Park and read the theatre page in the *Times*, my ukulele next to me. I felt like a true denizen of show business, and I breathed in Times Square like perfume. A cup of hot chocolate steamed in my hand. *Producer Jed Harris arrives today on the Normandie with plans for his fall season. It can be said now that these plans include Thornton Wilder's latest play 'Our Town.' Next Monday night Ed Wynn will open the Philadelphia tryout of 'Hooray for What!' a new musical satire with songs by Harold Arlen and E.Y. Harburg.*

Church bells were ringing somewhere.

Previewing next Saturday afternoon at Labor Stage, 'Pins and Needles'—a satirical revue by Marc Blitzstein,

Arthur Arent, Harold J. Rome, and Emanual Eisenberg.

I picked up my ukulele and my script for *Caesar*, and, walking down the steps of the park, I felt in direct contact with a fantastically lucky universe, felt it hard under my feet. And, yes, I knew people were still desperate to find work, and people were still bombing each other in Shanghai, and the world could be dark and terrible—*but not that afternoon.* Not for that second. That second it was sunshine rising beyond the clouds. It was Orson Welles and the taste of hot chocolate and the smell of the *Times* ink and the face of every extraordinary woman passing on Sixth Avenue.

Taped to the box office window of the Mercury was the Hirschfeld cartoon that had run in Sunday's paper. The drawing showed a brooding, hooded-eyed Welles in black jacket and black tie staring at the sprawled body of Joe Holland. Caricatures of Gabel and Coulouris stood nearby. In the background, a circle of silhouettes stood shoulder to shoulder, and the caption read: *The death of Caesar as they will start doing it Thursday at the newly christened Mercury Theatre.*

About ten men and women waited in line outside the box office.

I pushed up the brim of my hat, and as slowly as I could, entered the main doors of the theatre. A woman turned to look at me.

There was shouting—Welles and Houseman arguing

in the lobby.

"I'm sorry," said Welles, holding up his hands. "I have a commitment to Joe Ainley. He moved the whole goddamned radio show to New York just for me. It will *not* take more than an hour."

"Your primary commitment is to the Mercury!" said Houseman.

"You'll get your Thursday opening."

"Do you have any idea how much we have riding on this, Orson?"

Welles put his arm around my shoulder. "Don't go, Junior. We'll rehearse in the cab."

Now Welles, Houseman, and I were all walking out the front door of the theatre. A few people on line recognized Welles.

"Orson, for the last time, we need you here *now*. We need every bit of your energy directed toward the Mercury."

A cab stood waiting in front of the theatre.

"Get in, Junior," said Welles. Then he turned to Houseman. "One hour. Have Ash run through the whole show while I'm gone."

"Don't do this to me, Orson."

"This is *network*, John. If the whole goddamn country knows who Orson Welles is, then that can't be bad for the Mercury, can it? 485 Madison Avenue!"

We headed uptown.

"I'm absolutely *starving* to death." He lit his cigar. "Well, Junior, it's Monday, and we haven't had the Bad Luck Thing yet. I'm a little worried."

"The Bad Luck Thing?"

"An old theatrical superstition. You need to have the Bad Luck Thing *before* you open. If you don't, then opening night *becomes* the Bad Luck Thing."

"You believe that?"

"I've seen it," said Welles darkly. "And this time it's making me afraid. It's the one hurdle we haven't passed."

"People have fallen down the—"

"No. Deeper than that. More sinister. It's a malevolent spirit that must be exorcised. But you pray it happens before the opening. If it doesn't...."

"How will you know?"

"You'll know. Everybody will...." He looked at me. "So tell me about you, Junior. What's the story of your life?"

"Well—" I began.

"Do you know Booth Tarkington's *The Magnificent Ambersons?*" Welles unsnapped his briefcase and removed a well-thumbed hardback copy of the book. "Tarkington was a friend of my father. Based the character of Eugene, the inventor, on my father. My father died when I was fifteen." He puffed on his cigar. "*Ambersons* is about how *everything* gets taken away from you." He opened the book, which was inked with crossed-out pages. "I've been adapting it for radio. Did you hear my *Les Misérables* in August? Sensational reviews and the worst goddamn Crosleys in radio history!" He laughed, and I realized, once again, I was a totally irrelevant element in the conversation. But still he was riveting. "Listen to this. Pure American poetry." He pointed to an illustration in the novel: two well-dressed men holding canes and gloves were speaking to each other in a train station. A large valise lay on the ground behind them. In the upper right-hand corner you could make out departure times for the trains.

Welles began to read in his deepest and most resonant voice—even the taxi driver turned around to look; you could *feel* his voice shake your bones—and instantly he had transformed himself into someone else. His accent was Midwest; his rhythm slangy, whimsical, wistful.

"'I may not see you again, Georgie,'" said Welles to me as if we had acted this scene hundreds of times. "'It's quite probable that from this time on we'll only know each other by letter. Well, it's an odd way to be saying goodbye: one wouldn't have thought it, even a few years ago....

"'We can't ever tell what will happen at all, can we? Once I stood where we're standing now, to say goodbye to a pretty girl...I was *wild* about her.... In fact, we decided we couldn't live without each other, and we were to be married. But she had to go abroad first with her father, and when we came to say goodbye we knew we wouldn't see each other for almost a year. I thought I couldn't live through it. And she stood here crying.'"

Welles's voice had grown quiet.

"'Well, I don't even know where she lives now, or if she *is* living—and I only happen to think of her sometimes when I'm here at the station waiting for a train. If she ever thinks of me at all she probably imagines I'm still dancing in the ballroom at the Amberson Mansion.... Life and money both behave like quicksilver in a nest of cracks. And when they're gone we can't tell where—or what the devil we did with 'em.'"

We'd pulled in front of 485 Madison Avenue. "Come on up with me," said Welles. "You can learn everything there is to know about radio in an hour."

He stopped to buy a newspaper in the lobby, and now we were striding toward the elevators, Welles in that dark blue suit, looking brash, handsome, successful, talented—everything I believed I wanted to be.

"Excuse me," said a young man stepping from behind a column. He was wearing a black sweater and black trousers. "But aren't you Orson Welles?"

Welles glanced up warily.

"I saw you as Tybalt in *Romeo and Juliet* last year."

Welles nodded graciously, whispered "Thank you." He turned to the elevator operator. "Twenty-two, please."

"One minute of your time is all I need, Mr. Welles," said the young man, getting into the elevator with us. "One minute."

"The sad truth is that I don't have one minute."

"And the sad truth is that I'm trying to get work as an actor."

"I appreciate your dilemma, but I'm not in a position to—"

"Just hear what I have to say for *one* minute."

"On what floor do you have business?" the elevator operator asked the young man.

"I'm talking to Mr. Welles."

"Look," said Welles. "Drop off a photo and a résumé at my office. That's all I can do for you. Twenty-two, please."

"Please step outside," said the elevator operator.

"All I want—"

He forced the young man out and closed the sliding metal doors in front of him. The young man was now shouting: "'Friends, Romans, countrymen! Lend me your—'"

The door closed.

Welles shook his head. "Everywhere I go they start reciting. In restaurants, bathrooms. Christ, the guy who shines my shoes starts auditioning!"

We walked down a corridor and through an open

door that said COLUMBIA BROADCASTING STUDIO ONE.

"Mr. Welles?" A young woman was waiting for us. She was stylishly dressed in a man's houndstooth sport jacket and white shirt. "I'm afraid we're going to have to ask your friend to wait out here during the recording; Mr. Ainley's very strict—"

"He's my biographer," said Welles, putting his arm around my shoulder. "I've already cleared it with Joe. Let's get started—your name is?"

"Lorelei Lathrop."

We were heading swiftly down a corridor lined with electrical cables taped to the floor.

"That may very well be the most musically perfect name I've ever heard."

She smiled and pulled open a door that read TALENT ONLY in large black lettering.

"Something so graceful in the way you move, too," said Welles. "You're a dancer, aren't you?"

"I studied ballet."

"You've seen Jack Holland and June Hart at the Ritz-Carlton?"

"No—"

"My God, if you love dance you *must* see them. Will you let me take you tonight?"

Pounce, Brutus.

In the studio the small orchestra was running through its cues. The principal actors and actresses stood before two floor microphones. Three men in front of a sound-effects table were trying out buzzers.

I was told to sit quietly on a metal folding chair near the control room door. Lorelei Lathrop handed me a copy of the script. It was the first radio script I had ever actually held in my hands—twenty-three multigraphed pages. *The First Nighter—program #377—"A Late Edition for Love" by Anthony Wayne. Sponsor: Campana Cosmetics.*

A voice came over the overhead speaker: "Let's run it through, ladies and gentlemen, and keep it fast and light. Eric, watch the timing. We'll be cutting an acetate to hear what we've got. Orson, you want to run through your scenes first? We've been rehearsing without you."

"Not necessary," said Welles. He lit a fresh cigar. "What do you want for Van Doren? Gruff and abrasive? Sort of *Front Page?*"

"With a little heart in it," said the director.

"Naturally," said Welles.

And so without any more rehearsing than that, somebody was counting down—*three, two, one*—and suddenly the Eric Sagerquist Orchestra was playing "Neapolitan Nights," the theme song I'd heard a hundred times, but now I wasn't sitting in my bedroom on a Friday night; I was sitting in a studio on the 22nd floor of the CBS building, and it was happening in front of my eyes and ears—the music and these wonderful voices coming out of tired-looking people who smoked cigarettes and wore ordinary clothing.

A sound-effects man played a recording of crowd noise, which was augmented by live ad-libs in the studio. The announcer leaned forward and read urgently: "All of Broadway can feel the electricity tonight"—there was that voice!—"as we eagerly await the opening night of what promises to be another hit at the Little Theatre off Times Square. Already outside the theatre, a crowd of autograph-seekers and onlookers has gathered, hoping for a glimpse of some of the celebrities in attendance tonight."

Another man leaned into the microphone. "Have your tickets ready, please! Have your tickets ready! Good evening, Mr. First Nighter! Let's see: fourth row, center. Very good. The usher will show you to your seat for tonight's show, Miss Barbara Luddy and Mr. Les Tremayne in Anthony Wayne's romantic comedy about life at a great metropolitan newspaper: 'A Late Edition for Love'—featuring a special guest appearance by Broadway's newest star, Mr. Orson Welles!"

The orchestra went into an "overture" and the crowd noise subsided a little.

"Curtain! Curtain! Seats please, ladies and gentlemen," said the woman playing the usher.

The announcer leaned forward: "Act One of 'A Late Edition for Love' after this brief word from Campana Lip Balm."

The red light went off in the studio, and from some isolated booth came the voice of an announcer reading a commercial.

There they were: Les Tremayne and Barbara Luddy, looking short and dumpy and way too old.

Then the orchestra was playing "big city" music, and one of the sound-effects men was clacking away at a typewriter while the other made sounds of ringing phones by pressing what looked like a panel of doorbells.

"'Did you give it to him! Did you give it to him!'" said the actor who had played the ticket seller. Now he was a reporter.

"'Of course I gave it to him,'" said Tremayne. "'I'm just waiting for Van Doren to come walking out of that office, throw that story on my desk, and say, Runyon, my boy, this is the greatest story in the history of journalism!'"

One sound-effects man opened a miniature door; another walked a pair of shoes with his hands.

"'Runyon!'" yelled Welles. "'*Runyon!*'"

The voice on the monitor broke in. "You're pinning, Orson. Step back if you're going to—"

"'Runyon! This is the worst story in the history of journalism! If you weren't working here for free, I'd fire you.'"

I felt as if I didn't breathe for the next fifteen minutes.

Act Two. Phones ringing, typewriters clattering.

"'Your story! Your story! I'm so sick to death of hearing about your story!'" Barbara Luddy cried in that little-girl voice of hers. "'Runyon, it's that story or me!'"

Five-second musical link. Then just the sound of a clock ticking.

"'I need more *time*,'" said Tremayne.

"'Story of a lifetime breaking right in front of your nose, and you need more time,'" said Welles. He was puffing on his cigar now in the manner of some old newspaper editor. He wasn't looking at the script at all; he was studying Tremayne.

"'It's Marjorie. I'm spending so much time at the *Eagle*. I'm afraid she's going to leave me.'"

"'And what if she did?'" said Welles. "'You think you'll *never* forget her?'" And here Welles—astoundingly—put his script behind him, and, staring right into Tremayne's eyes, pulled his words out of nowhere. Or so it appeared. "'Look at us, Runyon. Me without my story and you without your girl. We can't ever tell what will happen at all, can we? Once I stood in Grand Central Station to say goodbye to a pretty girl. I was *wild* about her. In fact, we decided we couldn't live without each other, and we were to be married.'"

You could see everybody in the control room going crazy—searching their scripts for the nonexistent speech. But the director, wearing his headphones, was listening. He was looking through the glass at Welles; he had his hand raised for his assistants to stop talking.

The words tumbled out from Welles as if they were pure invention. "'When we came to say goodbye we knew we wouldn't see each other for almost a year. I thought I couldn't live through it—and she stood there crying. Well, I don't even know where she lives now, or if she *is* living. If she ever thinks of me at all, she probably imagines I'm still dancing in some ballroom somewhere....'" Welles's voice had become quiet. "'Life and money both behave like quicksilver in a nest of cracks. And when they're gone we can't tell where—or what the devil we did with 'em....'" He lifted his script back in front of him. "'Well, Runyon, you've got a tough decision to make. And I guess it all comes down to how much a guy'll do for love. And how much *will* you do, Runyon?'"

"'Anything I have to,'" said Tremayne, somehow finding the line in the script.

"'Then call that girl up,'" said Welles. "'And tell her what your decision just meant to your promising career here.'"

"'You mean I'm—'"

"'Yes, I'm *promoting* you, Runyon, *and* giving you two weeks' paid vacation, *and* a one-hundred-dollar bonus to enjoy yourself—now get out of this office before I change my mind. I hope you'll excuse me, but some of us have a *newspaper* to put out!'"

There was the sound effect of a phone ringing and being answered.

"'Hello! Van Doren here. Yes, I know we're late,'" said Welles. "'Just tell the boys in the copyroom it's *a late edition for love!*'"

The director threw a hand cue to the orchestra; they played the closing theme, the extras were applauding, augmenting a recording of thunderous applause, and the announcer leaned into the mike. "The audience is giving a standing ovation here at the Little Theatre off Times Square—and I've never seen anything like it. Taking his curtain call now is our special guest star, Mr. Orson Welles!"

The red light went off. Everybody was laughing. "What the hell was that!" said Tremayne.

"*I made it all up!*" said Welles, waving his cigar like a magic wand.

"God, I thought you were quoting something famous."

The director's voice came over the monitor. "Orson, I don't know what it was, but it was brilliant. It was the best thing in the script."

"You mean it was the best thing *not* in the script!" roared Welles.

"It's exactly what Van Doren needed—*heart*. Can you remember it for the show?"

"*The show?*" said Welles. "That *was* the show. Joe, we'll never get that performance again. You know that."

"Orson, we got some bad line readings early on."

"Not from me you didn't. You can record the others without me. Then get the engineers to piece it all together. They love doing stuff like that. I've got a rehearsal of *Caesar* I'm late for already."

"Orson—"

Welles waved his cigar in farewell, put his arm on my shoulder, and headed us out the door.

Eleven

Orson gave me money to take a cab back to the Mercury. "Tell them I'm going to be a little late," he said, and he got into another cab with Lorelei Lathrop.

Back at West 41st Street, Ash, the stage manager, was running the rehearsal. Cotten was standing in for Brutus, and they were blocking the curtain calls.

Extras first, including me, last one on the end, stage left.

"Follow Hoysradt, people," said Ash. "Look at him when you bow. *Once.*"

Then the two women.

Then all the conspirators except Brutus.

Then Holland by himself.

Then Coulouris.

Then Gabel.

And, finally—the Boy Wonder.

Cotten came out as Welles. He stood center stage. "I'd like to thank all the members of the Academy for this wonderful award. I honestly feel that so many others deserve it more than I."

"Take twenty minutes," said Ash. "Hopefully

Orson'll be back by then. We'll run it again. Looking good."

"*Looking good?*" said Coulouris to the other actors. He shook his head gravely as he rubbed lotion into his hands. "My prediction? The Mercury Theatre will be out of business by Friday. Believe me, people in 1937 will not pay two dollars to see tragedy! They can see it for free in the streets. My advice, fellow Mercurians? Polish thy résumé."

Out in the lobby Leve was installing a new chandelier. I found Sonja up in the projection room. There the icebox hummed; the radio played *Vic and Sade*. And then the war news: *After a horrific battle of nearly three months, China's valiant defense of Shanghai seems on the brink of total collapse. All day yesterday Japanese tanks rolled up and down the streets of Shanghai, shelling—*

She turned off the radio. She was looking tired. "I'm sick of the war. Do you sometimes think these are terrible times to be alive? I keep thinking about that, what it means to be born at a certain time. Every day layoffs, plant closings. People scared of losing their jobs. It *must* do something to you psychologically, don't you think? To live like this every day?"

"I think things are better than they were a couple of years ago."

"I'm not sure I believe that at all," she said. "I think

that's just New Deal propaganda. Sometimes it seems to me as if the whole world is falling apart. And it couldn't possibly get worse."

"Well," I said, "at least we can content ourselves that during these tumultuous times we're doing something really important—typing up subscription lists."

"It's crazy, isn't it?" she said. "Times as hard as these, and people go right on doing what they've always been doing: putting on plays, getting married, changing jobs—it's kind of *heroic,* isn't it? They go right on looking for apartments, making their big plans for the future."

"You've got great eyes," I said.

"What am I going to do with you?" Then she looked at me in a way that seemed to seriously take my measure. "O.K., so tell me who *you* are."

"Who I am?"

"Yeah. And don't tell me about your high-school sweetheart—or your parents. Tell me who *you* are. What do you *want?*"

"That's a hard question."

"What do you *love?*"

She was seriously asking me the question. I felt my answer needed to be equally serious.

"O.K. I was thinking the other morning that the one thing that fundamentally interested me was...I don't know...*words?* The words of plays, films, songs—all sorts of words. It's the one thing I find consistently compelling."

She adjusted her hairband braid. "You know, I pegged you right from the jump as a writer. I kept asking myself what's he doing mincing around the stage?"

"Mincing?"

"You know what I mean—all that ego up there."

"It's exciting," I said. "I mean, we might have a show that closes on Thursday night, or we might have a show that people will remember for fifty years. Probably neither one of those, but *you never know*. That's what's so exciting."

"You romanticize everything," said Sonja. "It's odd being around you. It feels as if you belonged to some earlier, nicer time."

"And what time do you belong to?"

"The thoroughly corrupt right-this-second."

"Well, opposites attract—as they say in the divorce court."

"You're cute," she said. "My cavalier."

"*Cavaliere*," I said, pronouncing the word with the five syllables of an elaborate Italian accent.

She sneezed.

We walked together down 41st Street toward the Mercury offices in the Empire. There were newspaper trucks in the streets carrying the late editions. (*A Late Edition for Love!*)

"Houseman must be around, what? Thirty?" I asked.

She nodded, her hands in the pockets of her cardigan.

"And you're twenty?"

She nodded.

"What do you want to hang around with such an old guy for?"

She smiled. "And how old are you?"

"Eighteen in December," I said. "Pushing nineteen. Wouldn't you rather hang around with a vibrant, young *cavaliere* than some old, English, overweight—"

Pounce, Lucius!

"He's running an entire theatre company single-handedly and offering me a managerial position in it. What are you offering?" she asked.

"Wealth! Travel! Fame! I can take you to movies that have *all* of those things. Provided you pay for the movies, of course. What are you doing tonight?" I asked. I couldn't believe I'd finally found the confidence to speak the way I'd always wished I might speak around a beautiful girl. "After the show? You see, I'm learning to fight for what I want."

"Good," she said, and she turned down a corner of her mouth. "I'm seeing John."

"What are you doing tomorrow night?"

She stared at the sidewalk for a moment. She smiled, then spoke: "Orson's spending tomorrow night out at

Sneden's with Virginia.... He lets me stay at his place on
14th when I stay late here. I've got a key. So if you want,
tomorrow maybe we could go out? Dancing? Maybe stop
by Orson's apartment for a drink?" She looked at me
playfully. "That too terrifying for you, my young
cavaliere?"

"Are you kidding?" I said, completely terrified.

"Of course, we've got two previews of *Caesar* the
next day, so Orson's probably going to rehearse you 'til
three in the morning tomorrow. You might just want to
go right to sleep."

I held open the door of the Empire Building for her.
"Oh," I said, "I think you'll find that we *cavalieri* have
considerably more energy than you might imagine."

She laughed, and I thought: This is the greatest
performance of my life.

The alarm went off at 6:55. I showered and got dressed with my eyes closed to see what it felt like to be blind.

As I descended the stairs blindly, I could hear my mother from the hall landing. You could tell she'd rehearsed this speech pretty well.

"We've talked about this before. Your father agrees with me. Ten o'clock on a school night is as late as we will allow. Is that understood?"

I opened my eyes.

Rule #3: If you are wrong, admit it quickly and emphatically.

"Mom," I said, "I completely agree with you. It's *ridiculous*. It's unfair to you and to Dad. I've been working on my research paper on *Julius Caesar*—I've had to interview these actors—but you're right, the hours I'm keeping are *ludicrous* and disruptive, and certainly not conducive to my schoolwork, which has got to be my most important priority in my life at this point. We're in complete agreement on this. There's just one thing."

She closed her eyes.

"There's *one* actor I've got to interview this morning at nine o'clock," I said. "I begged him for this interview, and this is the *only* time he can do it. It's Orson Welles. I'm sure you've heard of him; he plays the Shadow on the radio. Anyway, this is *very* important; my whole grade depends on this; college depends on this; probably my entire life depends on this, and there is *no* other time that Mr. Welles can schedule it. Honestly, Ma, this is going to be the *last* time in my life I'm going to ask you to do anything like this. I promise." She looked up. "So what you have to do is to *phone* the school this morning, and I promise I am *never* going to ask you to do anything like this again; from now on I'm going to be the perfect son—but I need you to make this *one* call for me, and tell them that I can't come to school today because of some family emergency or something. You know, a death in the family—God forbid. Something like that. And this is the *only* time that I'm ever going to ask you to do anything like this. *I swear to God.*"

Her face was getting harder.

"Ma, you can say anything you want to, except 'absolutely not.'"

"Absolutely not," she said. "You've missed too much school already. And I'm tired of you lying to me. I got a call yesterday from the school verifying your proctologist's appointment? I told them it didn't exist. They told me they were giving you three days' detentions. I said fine, I agree with them."

"Mom—"

"I don't want to hear it."

"All right, I'm going to have Orson Welles call you himself. Orson Welles, the voice of the Shadow, is going to get on this telephone and tell you himself that everything I've said to you has been the God's honest truth."

"You're going to school—and that's the God's honest truth."

"Mom—"

"And Mr. Goldberg called up from the Rialto. To make a *condolence* call. What are you trying to do to me, Richard?"

I sat in Mewling's class thinking of nothing for the entire hour except how I could slip out of school. He read page after page of his faded yellow notes. I didn't hear a word.

I was called down to Mr. P.'s office and given three detentions. There was no discussion.

I stood outside his office staring at the pink detention slip, wondering if anything else could possibly go wrong. Welles had called rehearsal at noon—and it was already 9:30. I *had* to get out.

I was feeling more and more like an outlaw.

The bells rang for a fire drill, and the whole school

shuffled outside to the sidewalk. I met up with Kate Rouilliard and her sunburned ankles.

"Richard, I'm sorry. I put you on the list. I forged the note about the proctologist. I thought that would be safe."

"Thank you."

"I don't know why they checked."

"So much for my credit. I've got three detentions, and I can't possibly serve them. Kate, I *have* to get out of here today."

"I can't forge another note."

The bell ran to return to class.

"Kate," I said, "remember you once told me that you wished there was something you could do for me?"

She frowned.

"I want you to call from that pay phone." I pointed to the phone booth outside the school. "I want you to call right now and tell them you're my mother, and that I have to come home instantly. There's been a death in the family. My Aunt Minnie had a stroke. You're picking me up immediately."

"Oh, Richard, I can't—"

"You said you wanted to do something for me."

"I can't sound like your mother."

"Yes, you can."

"Richard, this is stupid."

We borrowed one of those cheerleader megaphones

from a girl who was passing by. (I thought it might disguise her voice a little.)

"Now you've just got to practice saying this," I said. *"It's no use."*

I rolled along toward the city feeling like some old-salt commuter. (Kate's performance had worked perfectly. "Water off a duck's back," she'd shrugged as she'd replaced the phone. "But don't ever ask me to do this again. We're *even*.") I knew all the stops on the train; I knew how to sit on the aisle with my ukulele next to me so I could keep a double seat until the last possible moment; I knew the right staircase to descend at Newark and exactly how much time I needed to make the connection.

Rehearsal had been called for noon, and I used the hour I had to spare to visit the Metropolitan Museum of Art. I somehow felt connected to the armor and the mummy cases and the old Greek vases.

I sat in a quiet corner eating a bag of peanuts and staring at those fragments of ceramic that once had mattered. I liked the soft sounds of the museum, too: the whispering, the footsteps on the stone stairs, the class trip of seven-year-olds giggling and shrieking somewhere just out of sight.

As I listened, I became aware of a girl wearing wire-rim glasses and a floral print vest, her hair pulled back in a George Washington, standing before one of the painted Greek vases. She held a mailing envelope in her hands and was reciting something under her breath. I suddenly remembered who she was.

"'Thou still unravished bride of quietness,'" she said. "'Thou foster-child of silence and slow time—'"

I called out. "Gretta?"

She jumped, and she put her hand to her heart.

"I met you in the Gaiety," I said. "You were playing Gershwin on the piano. We talked about—"

"Oh, right, the *actor*," she said, nodding, and she gave me a genuinely warm smile.

"I'm even more of an actor now. I'm starring in— well, I'm sort of *standing* in the Orson Welles production of *Julius Caesar*."

"I'm sure."

"I can probably get you tickets if you want."

"You're not kidding me?"

"I'm playing Lucius!"

"Are you serious?"

"Later. I'll tell you the whole thing. What were you reciting before?"

She glanced back at the Greek vase. "...Keats. *Ode on a Grecian Urn*," she said a little self-mockingly. "How can you *not* think of that poem when you're here?"

"You know, I was thinking the very same thing."

"That's the odd feeling you get in museums, isn't it?

The sense that time's stopped? Keats was obsessed with that—how certain objects defy time in some way. Like this vase. Civil wars and plagues and a thousand years, and still this vase is around. 'Thou still unravished bride of quietness / Thou foster-child of silence and slow time.' God, isn't that wonderful? That an object which manages to make it through time is a *foster-child*? An *orphan*. To have survived, but without your parents, without your world."

"Have you had lunch yet? I want to tell you the whole—"

She continued quoting: "'When old age shall this generation waste / Thou shalt remain, in midst of other woe / Than ours, a friend to man—'"

"'Cause I know this pretty good roast chicken place around the block. I mean, if you like chicken."

"I shouldn't even be here," she said, and she touched the small of her neck with her fingertips. "I'm supposed to be working on my play. I haven't done my three pages today. Or yesterday. According to my time table, I'm now 108 pages behind. But I finished a short story since I saw you last." She held up the mailing envelope. "Finished it last night at 3:20 in the morning."

The envelope was addressed to Harold Ross, the *New Yorker*.

"I've got my self-addressed stamped envelope folded up inside," she said. "I'm all ready for rejection."

"What's it about?"

"This museum! It's called 'Hungry Generations,' and it's just this sort of funny piece about this girl who goes to the museum whenever she's blue."

"And what happens?"

She looked confused. "What do you mean 'what happens'? Nothing happens. Why does something have to happen?"

"No, I meant—"

"The whole story is what I told you. It's a John Cheever kind of thing. You know, mostly *mood*. The girl goes to the museum feeling blue. She thinks about time and eternity, and then she feels a little better."

"Oh...."

She got defensive. "There's no *action* in it, if that's what you're looking for. God, can't you just be walking down the street, and suddenly you're happy—or you're having coffee somewhere and suddenly the distance to the door seems impossible? Seems the longest distance in the world? Hasn't that ever happened to you?"

"Sure."

"Well, stories can be like that, too. Why does everything have to have a big *plot*? All that melodramatic garbage?"

"Hey, I'm on your side, Gretta," I said. "I agree with you."

"Now you've got me feeling that the story's stupid,

and that they're going to reject it because there's no action in it."

"I didn't say that."

"Isn't this ridiculous? You give me one sour look, and now I feel the whole story's worthless. God, what's the matter with me?"

"Listen, Gretta, I'm sure it's a brilliant story. It's *exactly* the kind of story the *New Yorker* loves. You know, *subtle*. Delicate. And there's this girl I'm friends with at the Mercury Theatre—she knows practically *everybody* in New York. She told me she's got a friend in Ross's office. I bet, if I asked her, she'd get this friend to submit your story personally. "

"Would she do that for me?"

"If I asked."

"You're serious; she'd do that? And you're really going to give it to her? You're not just going to throw it in the garbage can when you leave here—or steam it open and make fun of me?"

"You're nuts." I took her envelope. "I want to help you. Look, do you want to get some roast chicken or not?"

"You know, I came here because I thought these urns would be lucky. I'm *so* stupid. I wanted to touch the envelope on one of these urns. I really thought it would help me get the story accepted. God, they should just lock me up."

"If you believe in it, then let's do it!" I said, and I ran under the velvet rope and smacked the envelope against a large Greek vase.

"Hey!" called the voice of a guard.

I laughed, grabbed Gretta's hand, and we ran down a staircase and out the entrance, practically falling down the stone steps, and out into the sunshine.

She looked around and said, "Wouldn't this make a great scene in a story?"

She told me about the play she was working on, I gave her the shorthand history of the Mercury Theatre, and it was one of those breezy casual mornings, in the company of a girl, that make just about everything seem possible.

I promised her tickets for the show as soon as I could get them.

She was reluctant to give me her phone number, and I didn't push it.

It was ten to twelve. I said, "Let's meet again, O.K.?"

I thought: Maybe it's true. Maybe if you're just yourself, then you don't have to try so hard. Maybe the loves and friends and miracles just come blowing your way.

At the Mercury, Welles was still working on the Cinna-the-poet scene. "I'm going to stage it like a movie," he said. "Like one of those German horror movies." And that theatre was *dark*. He'd extinguished every light in the place including the exit signs, and he'd lit one tiny bulb flush along the blood-colored brick wall—just a smear of light picking out the irregularities in the stone. The stage looked like an alleyway now, the ghost of some security light filtering down through a closed-up factory.

Lloyd entered in a shabby black coat and tie, completely back-lit—you saw only his silhouette, and you could barely make out a sheaf of white papers in his hand.

Then, one at a time, the faces appeared. The really scary part was that you couldn't see anything clearly— just the shoulders and the hats, the occasional pale smudge of a sweaty face.

Epstein, at the Hammond organ, held a menacing low note rumbling under the scene. It got your heart beating faster.

Lloyd spun around now with increasing desperation, searching for a way out of the net, and it suddenly seemed as if there were fifty people around him, shuffling in from the shadows, rising up the ramp to swallow him.

Cotten stood in his military uniform on the step above Lloyd, his face set hard and merciless.

"'Where do you dwell?'"

"'By the Capitol.'"

"'Your name, sir?'"

"'Truly, my name is Cinna. I am Cinna the poet!'"

Somebody grabbed his poem.

Somebody knocked the other poems to the floor.

Lloyd was screaming now, backing away. "'I'm Cinna the poet! *The poet!* Not Cinna the conspirator!'"

Heavy footsteps beat on the platforms: the shadows rushing in around him, swallowing him.

The bass note on the organ swelled.

Then *complete blackout*—the bass note cut—and the silence was filled instantly with one terrible scream: *I'm Cinna the poet!*

Then the organ crashed out a horrible, dissonant chord—like a fist smashed down on the keys—and that sound held, held, held until your eyes narrowed from the ugliness of it.

Then the organ stopped.

Welles's voice boomed out from the audience. "My God, what a scene! Again! Again! Let's see it again!"

I drifted up to the third-floor dressing room—a large open room that smelled like cigarettes. I had been thinking a lot about Sonja that morning: fine, noble, dignified thoughts that focused in near photographic detail on the unhooking of her warm brassiere, and the imagined smell of black licorice pouring off her naked neck and shoulders.

The dressing room looked as if it had once been a dance rehearsal studio: coat racks, folding chairs, some cracked wooden-framed mirrors on wheels. On the walls were phone numbers and signatures of the entire original cast of *The Melting Pot* from 1902! A deck of cards had been abandoned mid-game.

I picked up a box of matches from a table and did that trick where you make a matchbox stand up in your palm by pinching some flesh inside it.

I lit a few matches to amuse myself—thinking of the fire I had caused in my backyard. Hanging from the ceiling were some old sprinkler fittings. I wondered if they were even still connected.

Then I stood on a chair, and tried to see how close I could hold a lit match to one of the sprinkler fixtures before anything happened.

Nothing. I held it closer.

Nothing.

Still closer.

A *pop*—a creak of the old pipes. The nozzle was dribbling water—then a fizzle of an air bubble, and suddenly it was *pouring* down water on me, not just from the sprinkler I was standing under, but from all four sprinklers that ran along the ceiling.

What the hell?

The pipes creaked and shuddered again, and I hoped maybe it was over, but the water just seemed to increase in pressure. It was falling on the floor, the newspapers, the ashtrays—four fountains pouring down like lawn sprinklers nailed upside down on the ceiling.

Oh, Christ.

I looked around for some kind of shutoff valve. There was nothing. The pipes simply disappeared into the masonry.

I ran into the hallway looking for a shutoff. *Nothing.*

Now the sprinkler on the *staircase* was sputtering and firing.

Get out of here, Richard!

I headed downstairs at a run.

It was raining on the second floor as well.

People were hurling by me on the stairs.

"What the hell's happening?" somebody shouted.

"I don't know!" I yelled. "I'm soaked!"

I hit the stage still running.

Holy God.

It looked like some Radio City extravaganza!

Huge ballooning fountains of water were cascading down from the ceiling. The stage, the wings.

Hot light bulbs were exploding overhead.

"'I'm Cinna the poet!'" shouted Lloyd, who was already soaked.

Somebody screamed and fell through one of the open traps.

"I'm Cinna the *wet* poet!" shouted Lloyd.

"Cut the power!"

"Cut the goddamn power!"

More bulbs hit the stage in an explosion of glass and water. Pools of water were already forming on the floor.

"Keep the water away from the board!" somebody was screaming.

Suddenly every light in the place went out. But the water kept on coming. You could hear it. You could *feel* it.

"Somebody shut it off!" yelled Welles. "Shut the goddamn water off!"

Another scream—somebody else went down a hole.

I could hear Leve yelling in his thick Jewish accent. "I think there's a cutoff in the basement! But I can't *see* anything!"

"Turn it the hell off!" Welles shouted. *"Turn it off! And put the goddamn lights back on!"*

"We'll blow the board!"

"I said put the goddamn lights back on!"

"I'm not touching the board!"

"The board's gonna blow, Orson!"

Still it rained.

"Will you turn off the goddamn water!"

"I can't find it!"

I could hear ropes creaking. Lights lowering.

Somebody cracked his head against something hard and cried out.

Then someone had opened the steel fire doors out to the alleyway, and there was finally some light.

Then there was a great creaking and shaking of the pipes, and air bubbles sputtered through the sprinklers.

The deluge ended.

The sprinklers hung dripping over the shattered lights. The soaked floor. The back wall darkened with running water. The actors stood with their hair and costumes soaked.

"Look at this shithouse!" yelled Welles. *"How in goddamn hell are we going to open Thursday?"*

Leve came up from the basement, dripping in his white shirt. "I found the shutoff," he said.

I stepped out into the alley, where some of the actors were trying to dry themselves off with their handkerchiefs. *Don't say anything, Richard,* I kept repeating to myself. *You can't tell even one person on earth about this. This had nothing to do with you.*

I commiserated and laughed with the others. I made a great show of drying myself. Inside you could hear Welles screaming: "Clean this toilet up!"

They're going to find out and I'm fired. They're going to make me pay and—

"Welcome to the Mercury pool party," said Cotten.

"Buckets and rags!" came Welles's voice from the stage.

And I could hear the actors around me:

"Who started it?"

"Leve says the lights were hanging too close to the sprinklers—we've got to lower the whole light bar by two feet."

"And re-aim all the lights?"

"We'll *never* open on time," said Coulouris. He wiped his face with his handkerchief.

Now lights were coming back on inside.

"The only way we can clean this up is if everybody gets on his knees!" Welles was shouting. "Anyone not on the ground with a rag in his hand in two minutes will be fired. We're under martial law! Clean the theatre seats first! Come on, you no-acting sons-of-bitches! The first two rows got wet. Jesus, that's all we need—a dozen critics with wet asses! And somebody get more goddamn rags."

I grabbed a rag and disappeared under the first-row seats.

There's no way anybody can pin this on me. There's no—

Suddenly Hoysradt was standing center stage calling for Welles, holding something in his hand. "There was a chair pulled under the sprinkler on the third floor," he announced loudly, grandly. "*These* were on the floor next to it."

In his hand was a box of matches.

The place went silent.

Drip. Drip.

"*Sabotage!*" spat out Welles. He walked center stage, his face red with fury. Of course, with Welles you never knew how much was genuine emotion and how much was just an actor relishing a star turn. "It's not enough that I work without sleep in this theatre, pour every dollar I make into it! But now this. *Sabotage!* Someone deliberately and maliciously attempting to wreck my show. All right, I want to know who is responsible! Whoever did this—front and center!" He pointed to the stage. "Front and center, right this second!"

No one moved.

"*Treachery!*" shouted Welles. He pointed out into the darkness. "Whoever did this will never work in New York again. *Never!* I will call police detectives. I will fingerprint this box of matches. I will fingerprint every single person in this company. I want his name, and I want it now!"

No one moved.

My hands were shaking so hard I stuffed them in my pockets.

"It couldn't have been us," said Cotten. "We were all onstage. It can't be anybody who was in the Cinna-the-poet scene. And that's everybody."

"Who else uses that dressing room?" asked Welles.

"Nobody except...."

"*Except who?*"

(*Top*) Richard (Zac Efron) reads *John Gielgud's Hamlet* on the train to New York. (*Above*) 'Wouldn't this make a great scene for a story?' Gretta (Zoe Kazan) and Richard (Zac Efron) discuss Gershwin.

'Wheaties': Richard (Zac Efron) plays a drum roll for William Mowry (Daniel Tuite), Orson Welles (Christian McKay), Norman Lloyd (Leo Bill), Joe Holland (Simon Nehan) and Grover Burgess (Patrick Kennedy).

'Mercury Madhouse': Sonja Jones (Claire Danes) fields calls in the theatre office.

(*Top*) Richard (Zac Efron) learning his lines in the stalls of the Mercury Theatre.
(*Above*) 'One of those letters that change your life': Richard (Zac Efron),
Sonja (Claire Danes) and the note from David O. Selznick.

The Mercury Theatre set at Pinewood Studios for 'Me and Orson Welles'.

'Dance, fool': Richard (Zac Efron) and Sonja (Claire Danes) on a date in Greenwich Village.

(*Top*) 'A god–created actor': Richard (Zac Efron) and Orson (Christian McKay) make a deal. (*Above*) Joseph Cotton (James Tupper), Evelyn Allen (Megan Maczko), Joe Holland (Simon Nehan) and George Coulouris (Ben Chaplin) on stage on the opening night of *Julius Caesar*.

'Orpheus with his
lute': Richard
(Zac Efron) plays the
ukulele to Orson
(Christian McKay).

Orson (Christian
McKay) as Brutus
and Muriel Brassler
(Kelly Reilly) as
Portia in *Julius Caesar*.

(*Top*) Orson (Christian McKay) and Richard (Zac Efron) perform to a full house
on opening night.
(*Above*) 'How the hell do I top this?': Orson Welles (Christian McKay) in the limelight.

'You told the boss the truth': Richard (Zac Efron) with Orson's card.

'I don't believe in luck': Sonja (Claire Danes) gives Richard (Zac Efron) a farewell kiss.

"Nobody."

"Anybody could have gone up there," said Lloyd.

"Sure," said Cotten. "There are chairs and matches all over this goddamn theatre, Orson."

"Leve says it's the lights," said Vakhtangov. "We've got to lower the light bar."

"This is sabotage!" insisted Welles.

"Leve says it's the lights."

"What the hell does *he* know!" said Welles. He was storming toward his dressing room when his gaze fell on me. He nailed me with his finger. "And where were *you* during all of this, Junior?"

I couldn't speak.

"You weren't onstage. *You* weren't in the scene. *You* use that dressing room up there, don't you? *You* did this! Confess it or I'll beat it out of you!"

"I was outside."

"You did it!"

"No, I was outside..."

"Confess it!"

I searched blankly around, my heart hammering.

Then I met his eyes. "Maybe...," I said, "maybe this is just the Bad Luck Thing."

Silence.

Drip. Drip.

Welles lowered his finger. I could actually hear him breathing. "Wait a minute," he said. He looked around at the dripping stage. The lights. The platforms. The soaked actors standing almost frozen where they stood. "The Bad Luck Thing," he repeated softly.

Then he nodded as if convincing himself of something.

"Thank you," he said.

Thirteen

Welles was shouting. "Faster. Jump on your cues, for Christ's sake!"

Blackout. Music. Duthie calling out from the back of the house: "'Caesar!'"

"'Peace! Bid every noise be still...I hear a tongue shriller than all the music cry—'"

"*Faster!*" yelled Welles.

"'Goodnight, my lord,'" said Gabel—his last line in the show. He made a gentle bow of departure.

"Lose the bow," said Welles, "'and goodnight, good brother.'"

"I like the bow."

"This scene is too faggy already. Lose it. *Lucius!* Faster."

I was leaping out of the trap. "'Here, my good lord.'"

"'What, thou speak'st drowsily?'" Welles stared at me. "Where is thy ukulele, boy?"

"I think some asshole doth stole it."

"Jesus Christ, this is some rehearsal," said Welles. "Skip this scene. *Cue the finale!*"

Anthony delivered his eulogy with the finale music

rising behind him, the lights shooting straight up from the floor. "'...His life was gentle, and the elements so mixed in him that Nature might stand up and say to all the world: *This was a man.*'"

Finale music up. Curtain calls. I looked over to see Lloyd at the other end of the extras. He had my ukulele in his hand. I gave him the finger as we bowed.

Then Muriel and Evelyn.

Then all the conspirators.

Then George Coulouris.

Then Martin Gabel.

Then, finally, the Mighty Orson.

"Ninety-four minutes," called out Ash.

"Rough," said Welles. "The big scenes are working pretty well—but we have to move them faster and watch the transitions; they're endless. Jeannie Rosenthal, please stay; we need to redo all the early light cues. We're using our best effects too early. George Coulouris, start the oration *lower*; you've got nowhere to go. Martin Gabel—tent scene—slow the hell down; we're pushing the river. Let the *scene* carry the baggage. Joe Holland, when you play that last bit, 'I am as constant as the Northern star.' *More.* And step closer to the audience. They've really got to *hate* you. Evelyn Allen, you look beautiful, my angel, but I can't hear *one* word you're saying. I don't know what else to tell you except that if you refuse to project on Thursday night, your theatrical career is over. And thunderdrum man? Much too loud; you're fighting the actors. Other than that, boys and girls, we're closing in on the son-of-a-bitch! Now, let's take the whole goddamn thing from the top."

We performed the show early that evening to about fifty friends of the cast. It was getting better. There was still trouble with the one hundred and seventeen light cues; the funeral oration was sloppy: Coulouris had tried to start lower, but his change threw off the extras, and we lost the intensity of the crowd scene. I had stood in the wings as Coulouris finished his last big line: "'Here was a Caesar! When comes such another!'" Then he stormed past me. *"Down the toilet!"* he said. "Whole scene down the toilet!"

"I thought you were fine," I said.

"I *was* fine," he said. "The *audience* was off!"

I sat next to Welles, played my song about Orpheus and his lute, looked out at the house, and I thought: Wait 'til my friends see this: Caroline and Stefan and Skelly and Kate Rouilliard and Kristina Stakuna and every other good-looking girl in Westfield High School. I imagined them all. And my parents and my grandparents. Wait 'til they see this! I'm onstage with Orson Welles; I can feel the body heat from his shoulder.

The cast lingered around the stage, and their friends all told them how wonderful they were. Muriel Brassler

complained that her costume made her look too tall.
Evelyn Allen sat looking lonely, holding her rust-colored
book. Cotten was talking about how he was going to nail
Evelyn before the week was out. "She's putting out
signals," he explained. "Very explicit signals."

Then the back door opened, and Sonja and
Houseman were coming down the aisle together,
laughing. She was wearing a burgundy cashmere coat,
dressed for going out somewhere nice.

I felt foolish to have hoped she'd really wanted to see
me after the show. To go dancing. Another daydream.
The truth was, I told myself, that the Sonjas of the world
didn't end up with the Richards of the world. That's just
not the way the play was written. The beautiful people
ended up with the beautiful people.

Suddenly Welles was gathering everybody center
stage. His manner had returned to that of an affectionate
teacher. "Now, all right, everybody, front and center! I'm
not done yet! Front and center, Uncle Orson's got a little
game for us all. It's coming together, ladies and
gentlemen, but we still don't feel like a family."

"Good. I hate my family," said Lloyd.

"Come on now," said Welles. "I've got a game I want
us all to play."

"At this hour?"

"I know what's coming," said Cotten.

"I still think it's a good idea, Joe," said Welles.

"Right now. Right this second, before you go home to your warm beds, every single person in this company is going to take somebody out for a drink. My treat. A *coffee* for you, Junior. Or whatever the hell it is you kids drink." He laughed. "Anyway, my treat. Five dollars a couple. This is the advantage of radio; they pay you in cash."

"Do we have to do this?" groaned Coulouris. "I'm exhausted."

"You—especially—have to do this," said Welles. "Anyone who refuses is fired on the spot. Aside from that, it's strictly voluntary. Now, there aren't enough women to go around, but we're very open-minded in this company. And we'll be choosing entirely at random." Welles handed me a stack of numbered *Caesar* tickets from last week's canceled opening. "Junior, give everybody one of these."

I began to distribute the tickets, and he continued his explanation. "Everybody takes a ticket," he said, lighting a cigar. "Then you rip the ticket in half and throw one half in a hat. Now all we need is a goddamn hat. Cotten, where's that stupid-looking chauffeur's hat?"

I handed out the tickets, and a beautiful idea was rising in my criminal heart. One to Cotten, one to Brassler, one to Gabel, one to Coulouris. Houseman and Sonja had walked to the apron of the stage. "You going to play?" I asked casually.

"*Everybody* gets one!" said Welles. "Including me. And when you get your ticket, tear it in half."

I handed Sonja her ticket, and, as I smiled, I repeated her ticket number, R-173, silently to myself fifty times.

"Where's that goddamn hat?" said Welles.

I tore offstage to find it—found a grease pencil on Welles's makeup table and wrote Sonja's number on my palm.

I returned with the hat and collected all the tickets.

"Now, I've got forty crisp five-dollar bills here," said Welles, "that I'm *determined* to give away."

"I don't see why we should be forced to—"

I stood onstage holding the hat, and before I could say anything, Cotten had volunteered to go first.

I thought: *Don't pick her. If there's a benevolent God in the universe please intervene here.*

He shuffled the ripped tickets with his hand.

Everybody was laughing.

"I'll go next," I said.

"If I get Lloyd, I quit," said Cotten.

"Can we start already?" said Coulouris.

Cotten reached in, pulled out a number, and read it aloud: *R-107.*

People studied their tickets.

"That's me!" called out Vakhtangov.

Everybody applauded.

"You make a *lovely* couple," said Lloyd.

"Can I pick again?" Cotten said.

"O.K., who's next?"

"Me," I said.

"I am," Muriel announced imperiously. She stuck her hand aggressively into the hat and picked a number. She read it out loud as if she were reciting poetry. "Number A-A-8!"

"That seems to be my number," said Houseman.

People applauded.

"Thank God. *Somebody* I can talk to," said Muriel.

"I better pick before all the women are gone," said Welles, and he plunged his hand into the tickets.

"Let me go," I said. "I have to go home early because it's a school night."

This got a laugh from everyone.

"No alcohol now, Junior. I don't want any calls from your mother."

Oh, I was all smiles.

I reached for a ticket, picked one, and read the number loudly from the palm of my hand. "R-173!"

It was gift night at the Rialto Theatre!

There was a silence.

No one acknowledged it.

She doesn't want to go out with me.

I read it again.

"R-173!"

Then Sonja's voice. "I think that's me."

Scattered applause and a few wolf whistles.

I dropped the ticket instantly back in the hat, then turned to Welles. "I probably should have held onto my ticket, right?"

"Don't worry about it, Junior." He handed me a five-dollar bill.

I hopped down from the stage.

"This seems to be my lucky night," I said to Sonja.

"Luck, huh?" she said. "Let's go somewhere we can get a good steak." She did her impression of Welles. "I'm absolutely *starving* to death! Can we go to Farrish's?"

"...swell."

I quickly calculated that my entire life savings on earth amounted to the three dollars in my wallet plus the five bucks Welles had just given me.

"And then, maybe, the Casino?"

"...swell."

"They have absolutely the *best* band there—I know the bartender; he'll serve you. We can dance a little, my *cavaliere*? And later, if you like, I'll show you Orson's place. Unless you have to run right back to Jersey."

"Are you kidding? This is an early night for me."

Fourteen

The steaks at Farrish's were huge, bloodied and charcoal-seared, and we tore through them as only two people who might possibly go to bed with each other could. I imagined we looked like one of those couples I had always watched in the corners of restaurants: the girl animated, long-necked, the guy in his black shirt and polka dot tie, his sleeves rolled up, totally absorbed in each other's presence. I couldn't tell you what the restaurant looked like, but I could tell you exactly what Sonja's earrings looked like: champagne-colored pearl drops on white gold posts collared with a tiny gold filigree. Her nail polish was pale peach. I could describe the shape of her small hands, that when she held her palm to mine, her fingers were an inch and a half shorter. I could describe her large, alert brown eyes, too, but for those I might need additional notebooks.

Red meat roaring in our veins, we taxied to the Greenwich Village Casino. I was spending every cent I had, and I didn't care. Let them carry me off in handcuffs. I just didn't want the night to end. Sonja wore a blue turtleneck and her burgundy cashmere skirt, blue socks, soft black flats. Other than the pearl earrings,

she didn't wear one scrap of jewelry: no ring, no watch—
just the statuary of her hands, and the beautiful planes of
her neck and shoulders, and the soft way her hair fell
behind her ears.

I was hopelessly outclassed, but I went with the
moment. I figured this wasn't going to happen again in
my lifetime.

People were singing along with the songs as they
danced, and I knew the words to practically all of
them—including the really old ones.

"You *were* born in the wrong generation," she said. "I
grew up pretty much in a house without music. But I
love to dance. I love it 'cause you don't have to *think*,
you know? I'm so damn tired of thinking all the time."

"I just love popular songs," I said. "I think they're the
great American art."

"Speaking of the great American art," she said, "I
gave that short story to my friend over at the *New Yorker*.
She says don't expect much. Was it written by your
girlfriend?" She batted her eyelashes in mock
coquettishness.

"Which one?"

"Dance, fool."

We had drunk white wine, and the whole earth
didn't feel quite big enough for me. We walked up 14th
Street in that strange dreamlike night. The air was

misty—every streetlight a constellation, every luminous sign a breathing presence—and the cars passed on quilts of fog. The lamps glittered back from the running gutters. A man walked his dog, and their shadows stretched out for thirty feet. A streetlight still wore a red, white, and blue sign: VOTE DEMOCRATIC! JEREMIAH T. MAHONEY FOR MAYOR.

I had my arm around Sonja, around her cashmere coat with its huge lapels and cashmere belt.

She sneezed. "I don't understand why I feel so comfortable with you. I hardly know you."

"That's the moonlight, I expect," I said. "Moonlight is cruelly deceptive."

"There isn't any moonlight."

"I know. It's a line from *Private Lives*. I've been waiting seventeen years to say it. Can I kiss you?"

"You're going to get my cold."

"Screw your cold."

"Well, we'll have to see about that."

She went up on her tiptoes, and we kissed. "How was that?" she asked.

"Cruelly deceptive."

"Do it again?"

"I thought you'd never ask."

We kissed again, a little drunkenly, warmly.

"Your hair smells like black licorice."

"I'm just a bouquet for the senses, aren't I?" She

giggled, and she looked up at me. "I'm a mess," she said. "I'm telling you that right now, Richard. I'm a mess, and I'm the biggest malcontent you ever met. I want whatever I don't have. I hate what I've got. I'm in analysis; John's paying for it. I just started, really. The guy told me that my mother probably didn't want a third child. I said, 'What good does that do me now?' I think what I really need is an entirely new head."

"I'll take the old one." I placed a hand on each side of her head.

"You can keep it on the shelf."

"I could kiss it whenever I wanted to."

"You can have it; I hate it."

"Come on, Sonja. Strangers stare at you in the street."

"They're staring in disbelief."

"You're nuts."

"This is an old problem," she said. "I've had it my whole life. I look in the mirror; all I see is what's wrong."

"Let's dance."

While a radio played somewhere through an open window, we danced in that empty street.

I should have seen right through you,
But the moon got in my eyes.

* * *

Virginia and Orson Welles rented a small, nearly windowless basement apartment on West 14th Street. It was modest: scuffed wooden floors, plain white walls, white doors with polished black knobs, the oil burner in the closet. The furniture was old: a bamboo bookshelf, a lamp made out of a mason jar filled with seashells, a bird's nest holding three blue eggs, a child's tiny painted wooden house, a wooden pillbox carved with a flower, an old handbag. There was Virginia's original art on the walls—oil paintings of farms and snowscapes. There were lots of books, plays mostly: Johnson, Webster, Sheridan, Wilde. And a small teddy bear sitting in a doll's chair with *l'ourson* stitched across its red vest.

Nailed flat to the dining room ceiling was an oil painting of stars as if they were being seen through the four panes of a window.

"Economy skylight," I said, pointing to it.

"You know the nicest thing about this place?" she asked.

"That it's got no heat?"

"That it's got no telephone. It's Orson's illicit retreat."

"It's freezing in here"

"I'll keep you warm."

She had opened the icebox and found a bottle of wine.

A clock chimed one half-hour past midnight. We sat on the sofa. The only light in the apartment came from a tiny lamp near Sonja. The radio played softly, dance music.

"Have some more wine," she said. "Where do your folks think you are right now?"

"When I phoned, I told my mother I was the one-millionth patron on the subway, and that my prize was a free night at the Plaza."

"Oh, brother."

"Even *I* don't believe myself anymore."

"She believed you?"

"She was so grateful I wasn't lying dead somewhere, she was willing to suspend disbelief until tomorrow. Then tomorrow she can kill me. You know, I'm actually beginning to feel sorry for her. I'm such a lying son-of-a-bitch."

"So tell her the truth."

I shook my head. "The Mercury Theatre is not her dream."

"And what's her dream?"

"My mother's dream?" I thought a moment. "Expect little.... Rake the leaves.... Make sure you get a regular check. Don't tell anybody anything good because they'll immediately take it away from you. It's a kind of *pogrom* mentality, you know? That any minute the Cossacks are going to break down the front door and steal the dining-room set—in New Jersey, no less."

"I like your dream better," she said. "Anyway, at least your mother cares about you."

"All mothers care. It's in their contracts."

She tucked her knees beneath her. "That's what I'm in analysis for," she said. "Trying to deal with my rage toward my mother." She took another swig from the wine bottle and handed it to me. "You know I dreamt last night that I *hit* her? That I struck my own mother. I felt *sick* when I woke up." And suddenly she was crying—serious tears—wiping her eyes with the sleeve of her coat. "Look at me," she said. "I'm an emotional mess."

Her hair had fallen into her eyes, and I brushed it away. She took my hand. "Don't pay any attention to me, all right? Sometimes I have to cry." Then she began crying all over again.

"Is there a reason you're angry at her?"

"I'm goddamned angry at everything," she said. She wiped her eyes again. "I have a lot of emotional problems, O.K.? I'm angry at myself; I'm angry at you; I'm—"

"Hey, I haven't done anything."

"You haven't," she said. "It's me. I'm Lady Rage. That's what my therapist calls me. 'How's Lady Rage today?'"

"And how *is* Lady Rage today?"

"She's glad to be here with you."

"Then what else is there to worry about?"

"Ah," she said with mock drama. "And will you be the rock I hide myself behind? The mighty oak to protect me?"

"The mighty twig sounds more like it."

She took another swig from the wine bottle. "You should drink more, mighty twig. It might loosen you up a little."

"I have to stay strong to shield you from the wild, wicked world. I think there's an idea for a really bad song here: 'I'll Be Your Orson Welles, You'll Be My....' I don't know, who's he in love with?"

"Orson Welles? A Narcissist's Love Song. There's a new idea."

"You and the Night and the Mirror."

"I like it," she said, and she rested her head against my arm. "I like you."

"Sleep if you want to, Lady Rage."

"Don't call me that, O.K.?"

"O.K."

I moved my fingers through her hair, caressed her right temple—a tiny freckle northeast of her ear.

"I'm trying to lose Lady Rage; trying to annihilate her in my work, in my life. But I tell you, she's a tough son-of-a-bitch to kill."

I did my Ronald Colman. "Togethuh we will slay

huh."

"Good luck, Ronald. She's a cagey customer. So wary of being hurt, she's been known to strike first."

"What's she wary of?"

"Abandonment, my therapist says. In all its symbolic implications. I have no father, you know."

"Is he alive?"

"Probably." She pushed herself more deeply into my arm and shoulder. "I'm like Orson that way. Another orphan of the Mercury. I don't hear you talk much about your father either."

"I suppose I don't. I understand Orson doesn't have a father or a mother living."

"Yes," she said. "Therein lies the difference. My mother still walks the earth."

"Do you talk with her much?"

"We try. It's usually disastrous. She's probably a bigger emotional mess than I am."

"Well, mothers and daughters: that's always a disaster, isn't it?"

"She's clinically depressed. Clinically an alcoholic. It's just one great scene of domestic bliss there. She and her unemployed boyfriend, Tex."

"Tex!"

"Yes, another strong male figure in my life. Another rock in the storm. Another emblem of enduring passion." She opened her eyes. "You know, I see the way

my professor at Vassar loves her little boy—he's four
months old; she brings him to class. I helped change him
the other morning, and, oh, you've never seen such
adoration from one human being to another. All she says
is 'Who's the wonderful baby?' and 'Who's the special
boy?' and 'Who's the best baby in the world?'—just
cooing and joy and the expectation of pure
wonderfulness for this tiny thing with its big staring eyes.
And *everything* the baby does is *absolutely* fine, you know?
If the baby soils itself, that's fine. The baby is kissed, its
feet are rubbed—and I'm standing there helping her
change him, watching her pour out this love, and part of
it is absolutely wonderful, and part of it my heart is just
breaking because I know I've never felt anything like
that ever. I don't think I even *can* feel anything like that.
That *pure* and that passionate. And I want to. Just once
in my life I want to feel something that isn't *me*; that
isn't *me watching me*. That isn't me *furious* at the world
because it isn't noticing me. Richard, I'm so afraid that
if I ever had a baby that's all I could give it—just this
anxiety inside me and this insane need to keep proving
how *terrific* I am." Tears were flowing. She wiped them
away; it made no difference. "I can't even talk to my
mother on the phone for one minute now without
fighting."

"I'm sure she loves you, Sonja. I'm sure that in her
own complicated way she loves you."

"I dreamed I *hit* her...you know, I want to accomplish so much; to be so much—and I feel her pulling me down—and I hear her *self-righteousness* and her *defensiveness* and her *terror*—it doesn't stop; whatever I do—and I want so much to get *past* her—to get past who I was as this scared, needy kid—and at the same time I need her approval so much. It feels like on some level she *resents* my success. Resents that I got away." Her face was distorted with tears. "We're still these needy, pathetic children, aren't we? Do we ever get beyond that?"

"Probably not."

She wiped her eyes. "I'm not looking for an answer; I just need to cry. Look, I'm wrecking this coat. I'm going to wash up and find a nightgown. When I cry I feel so weak. I feel as if somebody was bleeding me. There's pajamas, I think, around here, too, if you want to stay."

"Am I spending the night?"

She kissed my head.

In that almost-dark apartment, I got dressed in Orson's red pajamas; she put on Virginia's white nightgown.

"They don't mind we're doing this?" I asked. My heart was racing.

"Well, I don't plan on telling them, do you? We can leave the stuff in the hamper," she said. "Somebody comes in once a week to clean."

"Beautiful night," I said, pointing to the painting of the stars on the living room ceiling.

She stood in front of me and looked up at the stars. I put my arms around her. Then she broke away and shut off the last remaining light.

I could hear her walk into the bedroom.

I stood in the living room.

I was so scared I could actually feel the blood pulsing through my hands.

"I guess I'll sleep on the sofa," I heard my voice saying.

Her voice came from the dark bedroom. Four words.

"Richard, come in here."

Wednesday, November 10
Fifteen

I wore Orson's robe; Sonja wore nothing at all, and we drank our coffees standing in that tiny kitchen with its yellow countertop. It was 7:30 in the morning. She was eating a piece of chocolate she'd found in the icebox. Then she filled her palm with water from the sink and drank from it as if it were a tiny cup. She smiled when she saw me watching. "Ha!" she said. She took another sip from her palm, smacked her lips heartily, her eyes full of sly charm. The radio played softly.

She took another bite of chocolate and then kissed me.

"You taste like chocolate," I said.

She kissed my white undershirt, leaving a perfectly formed print of her lips made out of chocolate.

"Don't wash it off," she said. "Now you can't forget me."

I looked at her eyes, her body, her bare feet, and I thought: How on earth could I ever forget you?

I sneezed.

* * *

She showered, got dressed, and was heading out the
door. "I'll see you over at the Mercury; I've got a million
calls to make. And don't worry I'll call your school and
tell them that you're working with Orson Welles. I can
be *very* persuasive." She smiled and pointed to the
chocolate kiss on my shirt. "That'll be like me kissing
you all day."

Quadruple space.

I got dressed. She made a plateful of cinnamon toast,
and we carried it up to the roof.

Below you could hear the city waking; the rain had
cleared; the sky was white-gray, shadowless.

"Now you're going to tell me you knew this was
going to happen?" I asked, and I bit into my cinnamon
toast triangle.

"I was pret-ty sure."

"Regrets?"

"None that a friend wouldn't forgive," she said in her
best Ronald Colman.

"Then I forgive you."

I wanted to ask: *Did I do all right?* But I was pret-ty
sure I hadn't. I mean, I hadn't messed up *entirely*, but my

amateur standing was grievously apparent. (*And grievously hath Caesar answered it.*) What was also apparent to me was that it wasn't sex she really wanted anyway. I wasn't sure what it was—maybe somebody to adore her; somebody she could hug; somebody she could fall apart in front of; somebody she didn't have to bargain with.

"It's supposed to be in the mid-sixties today," she said. "Isn't that absolutely amazing?"

"I'm starting to fall in love with you, Sonja." I imitated her: "Isn't that absolutely amazing?"

She touched the back of my head. "I know. I'm feeling the same thing."

"Are we going to do anything about it?"

She thought a second: "We're going to open *Caesar*."

"I was hoping you might say—"

She held up a hand. "We're pushing the river. Orson's right about that, Richard. You can't force *anything*."

"Of course, Orson's right," I said. "He's right about everything. It's infuriating."

"I think it's kind of thrilling. Watching him turning into a star right in front of your eyes."

"You know what's strange?" I said. "I'm in his show; I'm sleeping in his pajamas; I'm around him half the day. I feel as if, sometimes—I don't know—as if I *am* him."

"That's the pull of every great star, isn't it? The

feeling that you're participating in their lives. It doesn't make any sense, but there it is. That static charge on the back of your neck. John said he felt it the first second he saw Orson."

"For these past few days I've felt as if this whole city *belonged* to me, as if all of New York were this enormous stage set, and somebody said to me: *Richard, it's all yours to play with*. I'm feeling so damn *alive*. Like I'm breathing some substance that didn't even exist last week. All this, and I'm down to my last thirty-five cents." I had pulled out my wallet to check on my exuberantly dwindling capital. I took out my driver's license. "You know, there's a place on the back here you're supposed to send in if you make a mistake on your name and address? I'm thinking about mailing it, and telling them my middle name is Orson. I don't think you need a lawyer to change your middle name, do you? *Richard Orson Samuels*. Do you like that? I think I really am going to change it. Richard Orson Samuels."

She left for the Mercury, but I stayed on the roof for a while. I breathed in the city: its warming wind, its noise. And I was one young man on a roof who had just spent the night with a beautiful woman. My skin smelled like Sonja, and my shirt collar smelled like Sonja, and the air around me smelled like Sonja, and the sunlight suggested winter and hard days to come, but we would all survive somehow, and the seasons were bigger than any of us anyway—and we were all tumbling along on the breeze of something enormous and eternal and gloriously busy.

I thought maybe that's what roofs were for: to pull you up high enough to feel the totality of it all, while the ambulance sirens sang below.

Before I left the apartment, I swiped one of Orson's cigars, and as I walked uptown I struck a few Orson-like poses in the shop windows. I was so impressed by my own reflection that two workmen nearly crushed me to death with a huge wooden crate they were carrying. "Goddamn-sons-of-*bitches!*" I shouted, waving my cigar, and I stalked off down the stage-set of a sidewalk.

When I waited for the lights to change I asked myself: Which foot would Orson lead with? When I saw four men standing around waiting for a job agency to open, I thought: How would Orson stage this? How would he arrange the men? How would he light it? Were they friends or just four strangers outside a locked door? Which guy had the stammer? Which guy had the sense of humor? Which guy was hungry?

All of New York felt like my paintbox. There was a sonnet in every high-heel, a full-length play in every face.

On the sidewalk in front of the Mercury Theatre a placard read: PREVIEW TODAY: MAT. AND EVE. BARGAIN

PRICES! It was really happening: two paid previews, and
then we opened tomorrow night. It was one day away.
The lobby posters read *Production by Orson Welles*, and it
struck me for the first time how much pressure must be
on Orson's shoulders. He was twenty-two and opening a
show to the most brutal audience on earth. You had to
admire the pure nerve of it—that he could say, in the
middle of a Depression: I'm opening my own theatre
company, and I'm the star!

There was a line of people waiting to buy tickets. I
sang "The Moon Got in My Eyes" loudly, hoping for a
few turned heads, then I walked with a studied
nonchalance through the stage entrance. *Take a good
look, you jealous sons-of-bitches!*

"Ma! Yeah, I'm calling from the Mercury Theatre."

I was up in the projection room/office. Onstage
below—ten minutes before the matinée audience was
going to enter—Orson was still rehearsing.

"What kind of a—"

"Ma! I've got thirty seconds! Look, everything's
crazy here! We'll be rehearsing all day and—"

"What are you doing about school? I told your
father—"

"Orson Welles's secretary is going to call the school
this morning. I was just talking to her about it. She's
going to take care of everything."

"But how can she—"

"One call from her, Ma, and everything is fixed."

"And your job?"

"I've got Phil Stefan covering for me for a few days."

"Richard, I don't under—"

"Ma! I gotta get out of here! Ma! I'm a star! I'm gonna be on Broadway! Everybody's waiting! I'll explain *everything* tonight. I'm going to be home very late. But I'm going to school tomorrow. All day. Don't worry. I'm going to hit those books like you never saw. Ma! You're the greatest mother in the world!"

I thought to myself: Is there even school tomorrow? It would be Armistice Day. I didn't know anything anymore. All I knew was this theatre.

Oh, we were *hot!* The place was packed—682 faces straining forward in their seats to catch every word.

The big "secret" that nobody was supposed to know (and which everybody knew) was that John Mason Brown, of the *New York Post*, was in the audience. You could actually see him: stout, pink-pated, glasses glinting, third row on the left. Apparently he had to be out of town tomorrow, and, God knows, he didn't want to miss an Orson Welles opening, so he had worked out a deal with Houseman to see it in preview so that he could still write his notice. And if ever any show in the history of the theatre was played entirely to *one* member of the house, it was the Wednesday matinée of *Caesar*. We practically hurled the show in his face. Even Orson stood four feet farther to the left than he ever had before.

Gabel roared:

Why, man, he doth bestride the narrow world
Like a Colossus, and we petty men
Walk under his huge legs and peep about
To find ourselves dishonorable graves.

—and he practically grabbed John Mason Brown by his lapels and shouted in his face: *For God's sake, look at my performance, will ya? Am I a full-fledged, son-of-a-bitch star or what?*

And Orson, the confused liberal, sat listening in his dark blue suit. Quietly magnificent. The magician who had wrought this masterpiece.

Oh, we had John Mason Brown right where we wanted him! And Orson had been right: the *speed* made all the difference. Even if you lost the thread of the poetry, there was something so relentless in the pull of the pure melodrama of the thing that you simply got caught up in it.

Blackout. Thunder. The conspirators entered with their flashlights—and we strained our eyes from the wings to make out John Mason Brown writing furiously in his notebook.

"He likes it," whispered Lloyd. We were standing behind the thunderdrum. "He only writes when he likes something. He *remembers* the crap." Lloyd rubbed his hands. "Wait 'til he sees Cinna! He'll piss in his goddamn pants."

Muriel Brassler—butterfly shadow firmly under her nose—was a riot to watch. She'd pinned back her gown so tightly that her breasts were practically ripping through it. She'd altered the neck about two inches so that there was a *lot* of throat and chest visible. And she wore the silver earrings and the silver ring that Orson had forbidden.

But she took her lousy two-and-a-half-page scene, and she made you remember her. She marched that body in front of you and said, "Look, even if you hate Shakespeare, you've got to admire my ass. Just think what I must be like in bed."

"I think Brown's got a boner," said Lloyd.

"The audience hates it," murmured Coulouris behind us. "They're bored. *I'm* bored!"

Jeannie Rosenthal messed up the cues on Cinna—the whole scene was played in too much light, but the acting was so intense nobody seemed to notice. For the first time Lloyd did Cinna with just the slightest hint of a Jewish accent, and when Cotten and the others began to physically knock him down and pull the poems from his hand, it made you a little sick with the echo of the anti-Semitism.

I was walking downstage with my ukulele/lute.

"'Lucius!'"

"'Here my good lord.'" My voice cracked with nervousness.

"'What, thou speak'st drowsily? Poor knave, I blame thee not; thou are o'er-watched. Look, Lucius, here's the book I sought for so.'"

"'I was sure your lordship did not give it to me.'" I was terrified, and my voice showed it. *Come on, shake it, Richard. There's one critic here, and you've lost your concentration—what are you going to do tomorrow? Pretend these are your friends out there. Be yourself. To thine own self be true. Calm the hell down!*

I was sitting downstage, leaning against Orson's right shoulder, singing:

> *Orpheus with his lute*
> *Made trees and the mountaintops that freeze*
> *Bow themselves when he did sing...*

I thought: I just might get away with this.

Blackout.

I watched the last five minutes standing behind the thunderdrum: the marching stormtroopers, the black banners adorned with the crests of Caesar that looked suggestively like swastikas, the stately funeral music played on trumpet and French horn—then the lights shooting up from below like the grand finale of a fireworks display. Coulouris stood there, lights streaming around him, a figure of pure light. "'This was the noblest Roman of them all.'"

I smiled.

Caesar was Orson's love letter to himself.

Crescendo music—and then the final blackout.

One second's silence.

Then tame but decent applause. Something still felt a little off.

Curtain calls. We extras bowed modestly.

Then the principals.

And loud applause for Orson—oh, you felt the power of his rising star then. (*The noblest Roman of them all!*) He was the famous one, the one they'd heard on the radio, the star presence who had pulled them into this old theatre.

After the show, people milled around onstage—everywhere the smiles, the hopes for a hit. In his black military coat and black gloves, Orson seemed happily out of breath, fully aware now of what he was about to bring to birth, talking to ten people at once, giving notes to the actors as well: "George, I'm begging you to play down the oration. I know you won't listen to me—but you have to bring it *up* to that level."

"Photograph, Mr. Welles?"

"Get my good side." A flashbulb fired. "And Muriel, sweetheart-darling, light-of-the-New-York-stage?" He pointed to her skintight costume and her earrings. "This is a masterpiece, not a Minsky's piece."

She sneered: "How long did it take you to think up that one?" She turned on her heel.

"And no jewelry!"

"*I hate this show!*"

"Junior?" said Orson with his hand on my shoulder. "You sounded as nervous as I felt."

He laughed. I didn't.

A photographer caught the moment.

Houseman was pushing through the actors. "Orson! A word alone." He pulled Orson into the wings, and I was close enough to hear them. "Brown loved the show!" Houseman whispered urgently. "He wants to meet you. It's a complete violation of every canon of the critic's art; it will completely destroy the objectivity of his review, and I told him you'd talk to him in five minutes. He's waiting in your dressing room."

Orson laughed. "Is there any other profession so deliciously fraudulent? C'mon, Junior." He walked me toward the dressing room. "It's too absurd if I walk in there alone, eyes lowered, waiting humbly for him to tell me how *wonderful* I was—so we walk in together— talking—and *then* he can tell me how wonderful I was."

Sam Leve came up to Orson with a freshly printed

Playbill in his hand. "I have to talk to you, Mr. Orson Welles. There's a mistake here, and it must be corrected immediately." Leve was genuinely angry, trying hard to hold it in check. "A mistake in the wording—my name has been completely omitted here." He pointed to the *Playbill*. "There's no mention here at all that I designed the sets and the lighting, and I insist that it be completely reprinted before the opening. As it stands now, this document is an artistic misrepresentation."

Orson looked at him calmly. "Every *moment* of this show is mine, Sam. The concept is mine. It's *my* work. It existed long before you came onboard. John'll vouch for that." The photographer was still firing away. "You did a fine job in a technical capacity, and I'm sincerely grateful for your help, but there isn't enough room to print the name of every carpenter and—"

"Carpenter!" said Leve. "You insult me, Mr. Orson Welles."

Orson turned from Leve and walked me into his dressing room. He altered his entire tone as we entered. "Now, Junior," he began. "I see the Lucius/Brutus scene in terms of a purely musical *retard*; we've had two very *grandissimo* scenes: the funeral oration and the tent scene, and what we're looking for now is *pianissimo*— shut the door, will you?—an interlude which—oh, *hello!* What a surprise!" said Orson to John Mason Brown, who had risen from his chair. "How wonderful to *see* you again, Mr. Brown. We met at the Theatre Guild luncheon. Give me one minute, will you?" And then Orson sat me down, and for three minutes, without a pause, lectured me how the Lucius/Brutus scene must be played *pianissimo*, and how the friendship of Brutus for the serving boy was the key scene in the psychology of Brutus. Yes, that scene and his brief scene with Portia, while musically *pianissimo*, and lacking the theatrical *crescendi* of the rising action around it, were vital elements in the music of the play whose whole theatrical energy was a matter of *tempi* increasing *poco a poco*.

It was the single greatest load of horseshit I'd ever heard—delivered with a perfectly straight face—and half of it in Italian! I listened and I nodded: the perfect performance of the disciple at the foot of his *maestro*. "What we need to do," said Orson, "is go over the scene line by line in terms of *tempi*. Stay here for a little longer. Now, Mr. Brown, I *apologize* for ignoring you, but I am still trying to tighten the performances—fine-tune them if you will."

"Fascinating to hear you work," said John Mason Brown. "I feel as if I'm getting a glimpse into the very crucible of the artistic process. And, as to your play, Mr. Welles, even in preview, let me tell you—off the record—that it is, quite simply, a theatrical miracle. It's as I imagine the Elizabethan theatre itself must have been: unimpeded with the trappings and hokum of four hundred years of hackneyed stagecraft. What I felt here tonight was a dramatic *immediateness*, an electricity I haven't felt in New York theatre in years."

"I only wish you could see it tomorrow," said Orson humbly.

"I saw greatness this afternoon—and a theatrical power and purity that we critics usually just dream about. Acting at a level that equals anything the Group has done, anything *anybody* has done in this city. Not a wasted gesture. Every moment, every scene, every inch of the play filled with the audacity of your imagination. And—as you were saying to this talented young man— what a sense of *music* you bring to it! The rhythm! The pacing! Your *Caesar* is, quite simply, an opera—an oratorio in which every note blends with every other to produce a symphonic totality of *tempi*."

Brown stood up to leave, but not before shaking Orson's hand twice more. Houseman had entered along with Sonja. They stood in the open doorway, and Brown practically repeated the whole speech again. "...the tonality, the *tempi!*"

After Brown left, Orson and Houseman looked at each other for a second. Then they broke into laughter. "Somebody go by the *Post* and slip that son-of-a-bitch five hundred bucks!" howled Welles.

"A thousand!" said Houseman.

"Quite simply!"

Sonja gave me a thumbs-up, and mimed a kiss.

And then Sam Leve was standing at the dressing room door. His face was red. "Mr. Orson Welles, we must rectify this, or else you will have a lawsuit on your hands. And a union violation. A clear breach of contract."

He was waving the *Playbill* in his hands. There in the credits it read simply: *Entire production designed and staged by Orson Welles*.

Orson glared at the program. "It says 'designed and staged by Orson Welles' and that's exactly what I did. There's nothing to discuss." He turned back to Houseman. "Can we get an advance copy of the review? Do we know anybody at the *Post*? Maybe we can pull some lines for the poster."

The photographer's flashbulb fired off again.

"And my blueprints? And *my* set design?"

"What set!" laughed Orson, and he turned to me. "There's no scenery!" He turned back to Leve. "Do you want a special citation for no scenery? 'Bare stage constructed by Samuel Leve'?"

"Then I'll start pulling down the ramps I built on the *bare stage* right now," said Leve. "I'll start ripping out the platforms I built for your *bare stage*, and I'll fill in the holes I cut. And you can really play your play on a *bare stage* and see what the hell you've got!"

"Sam, you've been paid," said Orson. "Frankly, I don't see what we're arguing about."

"My *name!*" said Leve. "I'm arguing about my name.
The money is *immaterial* to me, Mr. Orson Welles. I've
done artistic work here, and I demand the credit to
which I'm entitled. And if I *don't* get it, I will call the
union; I will close down this show—and don't think I
can't do it. I'm not scared of you, Mr. Orson Welles. I'll
rip out every platform I built. I'll repaint the back wall
the way I found it, and good luck with your opening
night, Mr. Orson Welles."

"The *Playbills* are *printed*, Sammy."

"Then they'll have to be *reprinted*."

"There's no way we can reprint them by tomorrow."

"Then I'm tearing down my set."

"For God's sake, Sammy, we *open* tomorrow. It's four
o'clock in the afternoon; there's no printer on earth who
can redo these by tomorrow. Be reasonable."

"*Reasonable?* Receiving no credit for my work is
reasonable? I'm tearing down the set."

"John, for God's sake talk to him."

"It was an oversight, Sam," said Houseman in his
best English-gentleman's manner. He touched Leve's
shoulder. "You understand that. I'm sure we can get this
rectified by Friday."

"Sure, put my name in *Friday* when no critics come!"

"My God," said Orson, "I can't believe you're pulling
this bullshit twenty-four hours before we open.
Everywhere I turn—people determined to *steal* my

show."

"Steal your show!" shouted Leve. The veins were protruding from his forehead. "Look at this." He waved the *Playbill* wildly. "'Entire production designed and staged by Orson Welles.' *That's* stealing, Mr. Orson Welles! You've stolen my work." He tapped his chest. "My reputation. For four years I studied at Yale, Mr. Orson Welles. Then I worked for the Federal Theatre. I not only designed the sets, I designed the costumes!"

"Sammy, you're a wonderful man, but any skilled technician could have done what you did, and nobody but Orson Welles could have done what I did, and *that's* what this *Playbill* reflects."

"It was an oversight," repeated Houseman.

"It wasn't an oversight," said Orson darkly. "It accurately reflects the credit for this show. But if you're *unhappy* with it, Sammy, then I'm big enough to reprint it for you. You want it to say that you played Brutus, too? You want it to say that you wrote the script? Fine. I'll print anything you want. But *this* is the *Playbill* we open with tomorrow night."

"Orson!" said Houseman. "Will you stop making it worse? The man has an authentic concern as an artist. He has his own reputation to consider."

"Go ahead! *Take his side like you always do!* You're another one waiting to steal my credit for this show! Good God, it's every man for himself in this company—

now that you smell a hit." Orson turned to me. "You know the only one I trust? This kid! C'mon, Junior, let's get something to eat; we'll work on our scene." He began leading me out of the dressing room.

"We're not done here, Mr. Orson Welles," said Leve. "You're the big expert on Shakespeare? Do you remember what Iago tells Othello?" And here Leve recited in his thick Jewish accent. "'Who steals my purse steals trash. But he that filches from me my good name robs me of that which not enriches him—and makes me poor indeed!'"

"Get the hell out of my theatre!"

Leve continued reciting, and his face was dangerous. "'Good name in man and woman, my dear lord, is the immediate jewel of their souls!'"

"The man is deranged."

"I'm going out there with my hammer right now," shouted Leve, "and I'm tearing up that set board by board."

"Do it and I'll have you arrested!"

Houseman moved between them. "We'll change the credit, Sam. By Friday it will be corrected. I give you my word as a gentleman."

"You *are* a gentleman," said Leve. Then he pointed to Orson. "There's a word in Yiddish for what he is—a *chazar!* A pig!"

Orson turned. *"I am Orson Welles,"* he said in his

iciest tones. "And every single one of you stands here as
an adjunct to *my* vision. C'mon, Junior, you're the only
one around here I can talk to."

I followed him out to the stage. Orson was
whispering to himself in an angry torrent. He was
enraged and nearly out of control. "Production design
and lighting design! Credit-stealing, son-of-a-bitch Jew."

"Don't call him that."

Welles turned on me. "I called him a credit-stealing,
son-of-a-bitch Jew because that's exactly what he is.
Does that statement bother you?"

"Yes, it does." And I realized as I spoke that what
filled me with an instant, visceral compassion for Leve
was that he sounded so much like my grandfather. They
carried the same prideful sense of their Jewishness. And
what so infuriated me about Welles was his near-
remorseless annihilation of anyone in his path.

"Then I'll fire your ass, too. I don't need *any* of you!"
Welles was playing to the whole company now. "Listen,
you want a career in the Mercury Theatre and in
everything else I plan to do, then remember one simple
rule: *I own the store.* You don't like the way I work here?"
He pointed to the back of the house. *"There's the door!*
Find somebody else to star you on Broadway. Now,
you've got something to say to me, Junior? Start talking."

I met his eyes. "All I meant was that you didn't have
to treat people like that."

He goaded me. "Go on."

"He's a human being; he doesn't need to be humiliated and demeaned to make your point. He deserves some respect."

"He's nothing," said Welles. He turned to the company. "Ladies and gentlemen, we open tomorrow, and I'm proud of every member of this company. Every single *one* of you has come through. You're a magnificent company—on par with any theatrical company in the *world*. And by Friday morning every literate person in this city is going to know who we are, and they'll be *lining* up for the privilege of seeing our work." He clapped his hands. "John! Sonja! Longchamps—my treat. I'm absolutely *starving* to death."

"I'll meet you there, Orson," said Houseman quietly.

Sonja gave me a gesture that said: *What can I do?* and she followed Welles as he walked up the aisle. He was still wearing his military coat and gloves.

"Sam, I am so sorry," said Houseman. "Words fail me. You see the way he is. He's not in his right mind. You can't talk to him now. Let me calm him down. I'll talk to him, and if I can get him to reprint it by tomorrow night, I swear to you I will. If not, I'll try to do an insert." Houseman took Leve's hand. "He's under an enormous amount of pressure. We all think he's unbreakable, but he's near the breaking point. If this thing fails it's all on his shoulders. He doesn't know what he's saying."

"He knows exactly what he's saying," said Leve. He was staring down the aisle.

"Sam, *I* know what you've done for this production. We all do. There would *be* no production without Sam Leve. And, believe me, even Orson knows that. You saw him in one of his crazy moods. Sam, he wants to be everything: the writer, the star, the designer. He knows this moment isn't going to come again for him—and he sees you as a threat."

Leve shook his head, stared down at the stage floor.

"He's young, Sam—talented and ambitious as hell. Forgive him that. When his mother died he was raised by a Jewish doctor; he adores the Jewish people: their compassion, their generosity, their sensitivity to the arts. Believe me, he's out of control now, but that's not who he is.... Sam, I promise I'll do what I can for you."

Leve finally met his gaze.

"Thank you."

Houseman sighed and hurried off to meet Welles.

"Mr. Leve, I'd like to buy you a coffee," I said.

His eyes were watching the retreating Houseman.

"What?"

"I said I'd like to buy you a—"

"Thank you."

He put his hand out, and I shook it.

"*Yiddisher?*" he asked.

Sixteen

We found a deli on Broadway, and with my last handful of change I bought us a coffee, a tea, and a baked apple.

We sat there for an hour talking about nothing but Orson Welles.

"He's a *mishugunah*," said Leve, shrugging his shoulders. "But he's a genius."

"You know," I said, "I was with Welles the other day over at CBS, and there was a sign on a door there that said TALENT ONLY—meaning, I guess, that only performers could enter that way. But I keep thinking about that with Welles—that it's *talent only*. That the only thing he has *is* talent—that all other human virtues: generosity, decency, loyalty—whatever—are missing. And because people are so hungry to be part of his success, they'll endure *anything* from him. Any kind of behavior is acceptable, no matter how demeaning, as long as he keeps bringing in success. I respect Welles as an artist; I really do. I'm in awe of him. But, as a man, he seems to me more and more a kind of monster."

"We live in a world where the monsters get their faces on the covers of the magazines, my friend," said

Leve, and he took another forkful of his baked apple. He smiled at its taste. "*Besser kennet zoyen*. Do you know what that means?"

"*Better it couldn't be*."

"How do you know that?

"Are you kidding? I had to do my whole Bar Mitzvah speech in Yiddish: *Meine taiera elterin und verte farzamalte. Zeit alla begriest!*"

"That's very good!" laughed Leve. "Listen, I have a theory about my work, about *our* work. I want you to hear this: 'As in the synagogue we sing the praises of God, so in the theatre we sing the dignity of man.' What do you think?"

"I like that: 'In the theatre we sing the dignity of man.'"

"It's what I believe. And all my religious friends who tell me why do I deal with all the *schmutz* and *dreck,* all the *filth* of the theatre? I answer them that the purpose of my art is to sing the dignity of man."

"And what does Orson Welles know from the dignity of man?" I asked.

He made a guttural sound of distaste. "Orson Welles knows from Orson Welles."

When we parted he said, "I thank you, my young friend, for the tea; and I thank you for the baked apple; and I thank you for being a human being."

"It doesn't cost anything to be a human being."

"Don't be so sure. *Gai gezint.*"

Welles had decided there had to be more musical underscoring, and with two hours to go before the curtain of our final evening preview, he insisted upon reworking the entire musical score. He stood on stage with the composer, Blitzstein (a little sharp-nosed guy with a mustache), and Epstein, the organist, and the score pages were flying in the air. Blitzstein would play a figure on the organ, and Welles would yell either, "Great!" or "That's the worst thing I've ever heard in my life!"

Epstein was shaking his head. "We need time to rehearse this, Orson."

"You'll be fine," said Welles. "You're a professional—every place I put an X, that means you play a march. Two X's mean a fanfare, and three X's mean a drumroll. Every place I draw a circle, just give me the sad horn melody. And the dotted line means thunder. Got it?"

I found a seat in the audience next to Cotten. Coulouris was sitting in front of us. "The word on the street," he announced, "is that the show is a bomb."

"The *Post* is going to give us a rave," said Cotten.

"We're supposed to be a classical repertory company—is that correct?" asked Coulouris. "Well, you judge a repertory company by the number of paid subscribers, don't you? The people who have *paid* for a whole season's subscriptions? You know how many paid full-season subscribers the Mercury Theatre Company currently has? *Less than twenty!* You tell me how we're going to make it."

That evening's performance was a mess. The house was good—about three-quarters—and they seemed as hungry for a hit as we were, their hands held to their lips in concentration, their brows furrowed, but the music was miscued, jarring, too loud. Drumrolls mysteriously began in the middle of major speeches—and ended just as mysteriously. Gabel was in the middle of "Three parts of him are ours already" when a trumpet fanfare began. He just threw up his hands in exasperation.

Now the whole theatre started *coughing.*

In fifteen minutes we had become the Mercury Tubercular Ward.

Welles exited from the long conspirators' scene, and he whispered to Epstein: "For Christ's sake go back to what you had! What the hell are you doing to me?" But the damage had been done: the fluid, seamless scenes of increasing terror, on which Welles had worked so hard, were falling apart right in front of us. We were bombing.

Things finally pulled together a little with Welles's "Romans, countrymen, and lovers" speech. He played it about three steps closer to the audience than he ever had, and it seemed to be directed not so much at the extras around him, but at the audience itself. He stood there shouting, *screaming* at them. "'Who is here so *base* that would be a bondman? If any, *speak*, for him have I offended!'"

He was something to watch—the son-of-a-bitch—a real fighting star, seizing the house and dominating the stage. It was Welles alone under the lights.

And he *had* them again.

He left the stage dripping with sweat. As he passed me he said, "That'll teach 'em to cough, the stupid sons-of-bitches."

We took our curtain calls to modest applause, but they couldn't quite forgive us for the first half. Everybody on stage was bellyaching about the music cues, and Epstein was defensive. "I did what you *told* me, Orson. One X for a fanfare, and—"

"One X meant a *march!*"

"You told me *fanfare.*"

Welles shook his head and walked off.

We heard his dressing-room door slam.

"John, are we going to fix the music?" asked Epstein. "You've got four union musicians standing here doing nothing, and the meter's running."

"Wait for Orson," said Houseman miserably. He pulled a stool center stage and sat on it.

"Let's go back to what we had," said Cotten.

"Wait for Orson."

"John," said Jeannie Rosenthal from behind the light board, "I've got that woman on the phone—she says she can do the spot work on the upholstery, but she needs to know what we can pay her."

"Tell her anything you want, " said Houseman. "We're broke anyway."

"We're running it through one more time tonight?" asked Gabel.

"Wait for Orson."

"And how long do we *intend* to *wait?*" asked Gabel with the same sharply enunciated "t" he used when Marc Antony said, "And I perceive you feel the *dint* of *pity.*"

Houseman shrugged. Then he looked around. He said to Cotten, "This is the essential Orson Welles moment, isn't it? Whole show in shambles. We open in under twenty-four hours. Entire vessel keeling over. Water breaching the deck."

"But wait," said Cotten in that same tone of mock-melodrama. "There is *one* man who can save us."

"*One man,*" said Houseman, "with the vision, the imagination, the—"

"*From the beginning!*" bellowed Welles, coming from the wings. "We go over the whole goddamn son-of-a-bitch show from the very beginning! And *nobody* leaves!"

"'Once more unto the breach!'" yelled Lloyd.

The entire company groaned.

* * *

It was sometime past midnight; Welles sat in the fourth row eating his second steak from Longchamps while he reblocked the crowd scenes. A radio, set on the corner of the stage, played dance music softly. (Welles said this helped him think.) In the news on the hour we heard that Jersey City Mayor Frank Hague had declared "I am the law!" in a talk on city government, and that Tallulah Bankhead had opened in Shakespeare's *Antony and Cleopatra*. No reviews yet.

"Ladies and gentlemen," Welles said to the company. "A moment of prayer—complete silence, please! Dear Lord, let Tallulah's *Cleopatra* be a total unmitigated disaster so that ours will look brilliant in comparison. Amen."

"Amen," echoed the cast reverently.

"Now, let's run through it again!"

Sonja was sitting next to Welles, taking his dictated notes. Houseman had been banished from the theatre for daring to question the usefulness of another rehearsal at this late hour. One of the extras stood in for Brutus.

Welles was at the top of his form—pleading, shouting, slapping his head, running onstage: "No, no, no—don't you know *anything* about theatre?" He sat back down in the audience, then cursed—leaped up again. He was going through an entire cigar every twelve minutes (Lloyd and I timed him). He'd smash the butt into the ashtray next to him and cry out: "Vakhtangov! Another cigar! And come on, people, pick up your cues. Do you really expect to open like this? Jesus Christ, is *anybody* awake here? Horns: too loud. Jeannie, lamp fifty-seven out, and I told you at cues five and sixty-five to turn off the goddamn exit signs."

"Orson," said Jeannie, "that's against the law."

"*I am the law!*" thundered Welles—and cracked everybody up, including himself. "Five-minute break to fix the lights, and then everybody back for the tech run-through. Then the real run-through." He turned to me. "Junior, *you* can go home. That's all I need—the goddamn Child Labor Commission shutting down my show."

Sonja met up with me outside the theatre. I had one foot up on the fire hydrant by the stage door, and I was trying to finish the cigar I'd stolen from Welles's apartment. It was two in the morning on a New York City street, and I was smoking a cigar!

"Don't you have school tomorrow?" she asked, her breath steaming.

I waved a hand dismissively. "I'm enjoying watching him work."

"The cigar's a nice touch," she said. "Part of your new image, along with your new middle name?"

I nodded.

"You know, Richard," she said, "Orson's going to be here 'til daybreak; he really is. I'm going to be here even later. I've got a ton of stuff to get organized. It's absolutely nuts for you to stick around here that long. You've got to get some sleep. You *open* tomorrow. Which is now almost *today*. These other characters can sleep all morning."

"I can sleep all morning, too. I don't care. School feels like another universe to me right now—an insignificant universe. And *I'm* asking you out for breakfast before anybody else. So don't tell me no."

I kissed her forehead.

Welles and Houseman came out the front doors. Welles was pointing to a place in front of the theatre. "Put the sign there: OPENING NIGHT SOLD OUT. It'll look good, and we'll paper the house anyway."

Houseman stretched his neck trying to get it to crack. "I'm going home to get a little rest, Orson."

"I envy you your rest."

"You can over-rehearse, you know."

"One more run-through."

"At this point, can it possibly make any difference?"

"This is when the magic happens."

Somewhere a churchbell chimed the late hour. They listened to its dying fall.

"'We've heard the chimes at midnight, Master Shallow!'" said Welles.

Houseman laughed. "Good night." He walked toward Bryant Park.

Welles stepped into the street to admire his theatre with its illuminated sign—and that's when he noticed Sonja and me.

"Are you still here, Junior?"

"He doesn't want to go home," said Sonja.

Welles took a deep breath of the night air. "'I know young bloods look for a time of rest.'"

"'I have slept, my lord, already.'"

"'It was well done, and thou shall sleep again.'"

"Really, I'm fine."

He spoke warmly. "Lucius, I love you beyond measure. You're the one person in this entire company who doesn't need any more rehearsing. Your performance, your song—they're the *foundation* of this show. And let me tell you something, on a personal level." Here he nearly whispered. "You are what I call a *God-created* actor. There are actors who will study their *entire* lifetimes who will never be able to do what you do with a look, a movement of your hand. When you're onstage, you *register*." He fixed me with his intense brown eyes. "I look at you, and you know what I see? *Images of magnificence.*" He gave my shoulder a squeeze. "See you tomorrow."

Welles held open the theatre door. "Sonja, I need you inside."

"One minute?" she said.

He left us standing there.

"Why do I have the unmistakable feeling that I'm being hustled outta here?" I said.

"You *are* being hustled outta here."

A cab passed.

"Orson wants to stay with me tonight."

"Stay with you tonight? That's—"

"Yes."

She said it without a flicker of remorse.

"And you're—"

"I'm not in a position to refuse."

"He's *married*, Sonja."

"It's more complicated than you think."

"Sonja, I'm going to say the stupidest sentence that—"

"Don't."

"I love you."

She actually winced.

"Wrong sentence, I guess."

"Richard, I have to watch out for myself. That's what my whole life has taught me again and again."

"You can't trust me?"

"Not one person. Everyone betrays you."

"I wouldn't betray you, Sonja."

"You just haven't had a good enough opportunity yet."

"I'm not Orson Welles, Sonja, but I would never—"

"You don't understand a thing. Sometimes you're so *young.*" She said the word like an insult.

"I would never betray you. That's something I understand."

"Goodnight, my noble *cavaliere*. Get some rest."

"Sonja—"

She stopped my hand. "Don't waste your energy. You're not going to win this one."

Then she smoothed her hair self-consciously and walked back into the theatre.

"You want my advice?"

Cotten had been standing in the alley smoking. He stepped out of the shadows. "Sorry for listening. Want some advice from an old pro?"

I gestured weakly. "Sure."

"Fight for her. It's what she wants. It's what she's hoping for."

"Fight for her, huh?" I looked up toward the MERCURY sign. "I don't know if that's who I am."

"And who you *are*—is that who you *want* to be?" Cotten tossed his cigarette to the sidewalk.

And he was gone.

For a moment I didn't know if he had really spoken to me, or if I had imagined it.

The white lights above my head which spelled out MERCURY were suddenly turned off. The wind blew a litter of leaves across the sidewalk.

It was late. I was bone-tired. And it was beginning to rain.

Seventeen

Tallulah Bankhead's *Antony and Cleopatra* was a titanic disaster. *Thanks God.* I'd heard Woolcott Gibbs on the radio that morning savoring its radiant awfulness: "Our old friend Tallulah Bankhead opened at the Mansfield last night in a production of *Antony and Cleopatra* that makes one understand exactly why every school-child hates Shakespeare."

I couldn't wait for the papers.

Meantime, I was bolting down my coffee and Fig Newtons—half-listening to my mother.

"And these people are paying you?"

"Not yet, but this could *lead* to—"

"*Bahlt.*"

"I can probably get a contract as an Equity Junior Member, and that would be twenty-five dollars a week, and then, after I work long enough, I become an Equity Senior Member—that's forty dollars a week. Think of that. Forty dollars a week."

"And how much has he paid you so far, Mr. Forty-Dollars-a-Week?"

"Nothing so far but—"

"And how much has it cost you?"

"It hasn't cost me anything."

"And who paid for the trains and the eating out and—"

"All right, I have—but think of this as an *investment*, Ma. An investment in my future as...some kind of an artist."

"Some big artist like your Uncle Sol is an artist."

"This is not like Uncle Sol."

"His whole *life* he can't keep a steady job. Another one like you, Mr. Big Dreamer. Always big plans. Had to be his own boss. God forbid he should work for somebody and earn a regular living. No, he had to be in charge, *takha*. Right away had to be in charge. Look at him. Forty-six years old, he still doesn't have a job. Doesn't have a nickel in the bank! Had to ask your father for money. And his poor wife, Harley, dragging her from one lousy apartment to another. He should be shot."

"Ma, this is different."

"You explain to your father how this is different."

"Someday, Ma, everybody in this town is going to know who I am."

"Sure. You'll be the one who didn't graduate from high school. And if I get one more call from that school today because you're not there, one more call, I'm calling up your friend Orson Welles myself, and I'm telling him how you can no longer participate. And don't think I won't call him."

"Orson Welles Meets Dora Samuels," I said, heading out the door. "A Comedy in Three Acts."

I met up with Stefan outside his chemistry class. He was walking out the door of the lab with his arm around Caroline. He yanked his arm away the second he saw me, and Caroline practically ran down the hall.

"I tell ya, people work fast in this school," I said. "You may be a lying, duplicitous, drunken son-of-a-bitch, but you're *fast,* you know? I've got to give you credit for that." And I realized, even as I was saying this, that my moral outrage was more theatrical than anything else. The truth was that *I* had just been unfaithful to her in a way I couldn't even have dreamed about a week earlier. But I enjoyed playing the role of the injured lover. It was a good, loud, Orson Welles part.

"Listen, bozo—"

"I'm not even debating this," I said. "Because frankly I don't care who you pounce on anymore. Jesus, it's the same story over and over again."

"We gave you the chance, little buddy."

"What chance do I have against guys like you? You guys *always* win."

"I told you, they want you to fight for 'em. If you don't, they move on to somebody who will."

"Then if that's the case, I don't want 'em," I said. "If they're that superficial and *prehistoric*, I don't want anything to do with 'em."

"Suit yourself, stud."

I watched Caroline disappear down the hall. "Did she even *mention* me at all? Did she act as if she was *remotely* interested in me?"

"We haven't done that much talking."

"Yeah, I know it's tough to talk when you've got her left breast in your mouth."

"Nothing's happened yet."

"That makes me feel *so* much better."

"I told you, stud, girls want you to fight for 'em. You don't have to *mean* it, for Christ's sake. But you gotta make the bullshit gesture."

"Here." I pulled out my two complimentary tickets for *Caesar*. "If I knew anybody else on *earth* I could give these to I would, but I can't think of anybody, so here they are. They're for that show I told you about, the one I'm opening in tonight."

"Tonight? Don't you want to give these to your folks?"

"Oh, yeah. Great. So my mother can show up with a garden rake. Are you coming or not?"

"Sure, I'll be there."

"And show up with Skelly, all right? Not Caroline, for Christ's sake."

He examined the tickets. "Yeah. This could be fun."

"And don't *yell* anything either. O.K.? This is Broadway."

I left all my books in my locker and during lunch I cut out the back door onto Walnut Street. I simply couldn't sit in class and pretend it mattered. *Screw the consequences.* When the show was a hit it wouldn't matter anyway.

Under a pine tree Kristina Stakuna was taking a drag on a cigarette; Joe Rutgers had shown up in his new Chrysler pounce-mobile.

"Kristina?" I said as I walked by.

She looked up narrowly.

"You are one exquisitely beautiful woman." Joe Rutgers looked up to see who I was. "I just wanted to say that to you once before I graduated." I held out my hands innocently. "No other motive here but pointing out beauty where I see it. And you are one beautiful woman."

Her eyes went warm. She laughed. *"Muchas gracias.* You want a cig?"

I shook my head. "Heading into the city. Want to get there a little early. Opening on Broadway tonight.

She raised her head in mild curiosity. *"¿Es verdad?"* She took another drag on her cigarette. I wanted to kiss her.

"*Es verdad*, sister," I said. "Me and Orson Welles." I crossed my fingers. "Like *that*. Give you all the dirt tomorrow. Got a train to catch. *Adios, lindita.*" I headed down the path toward town.

"*Adios.*"

And I left Joe Rutgers standing there with his big ape mouth hanging open.

Bam! Right to the body!

The wind was up. I pulled my collar tightly around my neck, set my hat at an angle.

I had some time.

I thought: O.K., if I don't get hit by a cab, I'm opening tonight in *Caesar*. If that guy in the doorway doesn't jump out and smash my skull in with a tire iron, I'm opening tonight in *Caesar*. If those construction guys up there don't drop a fifty-ton vat of cement on my head, I'm opening tonight in *Caesar*.

I had a cup of coffee and a plain doughnut in some little dive with steamy windows. I thought: O.K., if I don't choke to death on this doughnut, I'm opening tonight in *Caesar*.

I turned up West 14th Street. The clock from the Spanish Church was striking two. There was a cab waiting in front of Welles's apartment.

I heard Welles's deep laughter, then Sonja's laughter—and up from the basement steps came the two of them.

I hid lamely behind a street-sign pole.

Welles was reading aloud from a folded copy of the *Times*. "Good God, listen to this," he said. "'Slowly paced, incompetently spoken, badly edited, this *Anthony and Cleopatra*'—*Anthony* with an h! Christ, Atkinson can't even get the goddamn name of the play right! '...this *Anthony and Cleopatra* is a considerable trial of an audience's patience and good will.'" Welles shook his head. "Why don't they just ask poor Tallulah to apologize for being born? 'Her voice has none of the music that blank verse requires; she misses the rhythm of poetic speaking, and a large part of what she says cannot be understood.' God, this is priceless."

Sonja was breathless with laughter—then she spotted me. I had half-turned away, but there was nowhere to hide. She touched Welles on the sleeve. He glanced up, and then put his arm around her and headed toward me. He laughed heartily.

"Lucius, old man! What are you doing down in these remote parts of the isle?" he said. "A great night tonight! Can you feel it? Going to be one of those magic nights."

"May I have one minute alone with Sonja?"

"What's the problem?" said Welles. He lit a cigar in the windy street. "We've got half a dozen interviews this afternoon, a final tech—"

Sonja raised her index finger. "Give us one minute,

Orson?"

He shrugged and walked toward the parked cab.

She and I remained there. Her eyes shone bright and hard. "What do you want me to say, Richard? I told you what I was doing. I'm not sorry."

I heard Cotten's voice in my head: *Fight for her. It's what she wants.* But I couldn't seem to find the words. The hurt was deflating me.

"Isn't your wounded silence a little melodramatic?" she asked. "You've known me for a week."

"Sometimes you remember a week for the rest of your life."

"Then be grateful you had a week."

"And that's all there is to say?"

"Richard, you're a nice little kid from a nice little town. *Stay* there if you don't want to get hurt."

"I'm not a little kid, and it's insulting for you to call me one."

She moved in the direction of the cab, then stopped and turned. "Look, I warned you what you were getting into. People betray each other—and now you can add me to the list. I like you, Richard, honestly—"

"I love you. I'm willing to fight for you."

Wrong, wrong—

"Fight for me?" She smiled. "You don't even know me."

"Then *allow* me to know you."

She drew herself more tightly into her coat. "Orson is going to introduce me to Selznick."

"So Selznick makes this morally right?"

Worse—

Her eyes widened with anger.

Lady Rage.

"Morally right? This is 1937, Richard—I don't think the words 'morally right' mean anything anymore."

"To me they do."

"You're beginning to sound a little self-righteous."

I kept thinking to myself: *What would Stefan say?* "I would never do to you—"

She was furious. "You're so *above* ambition? So morally high and righteous? Great! *Quit the show.* You want to impress me with your nobility? Orson and I are so morally second-rate next to you? Great! Quit the show! Make a *real* stand. Make a *real* protest. Be a *real* man."

Now I was angry.

"You're not worth quitting for."

"I'm not worth quitting for—or you're just so piss-afraid of missing your Broadway debut that you'll conveniently look the other way? You better think hard before you start pointing the finger of righteousness at me."

Welles was approaching now. He'd been reading the newspaper, waiting, I imagined, for Sonja and me to resolve our little skirmish. "I told you, Junior, we're late already."

"Richard told me he wants to quit the show," said Sonja.

"I did not."

"What the hell is going on here, Junior?" said Welles.

And suddenly I knew how much I hated that asshole. "First of all," I said, "my name isn't 'Junior.' Or 'kid.' Or 'Lucius.' My name is Richard, and that's what I want to be called."

Welles turned to Sonja. "Get in the cab."

"This concerns me, too, Orson."

"*Get in the cab.*"

She did.

"Now what exactly *is* your problem, Junior?" said Welles, and he pushed me in the chest. "'Cause you're picking the wrong day to upset me."

I shoved his hand away. I wanted to punch him. "Sonja is my lover," I said.

"Your *what?*"

He laughed. And it *was* ridiculous, but it seemed to me a matter of pride.

"My lover. As in the-girl-who-I-am-in-love-with. And I resent your screwing around with her, all right? You've got a wife, for Christ's sake—a pregnant wife. This is *my* girlfriend. I'd like you to back off."

"Your lover, huh? You and half of Actors Equity."

"Shut up."

"You're angry at *me*, Junior? And don't you think—" and he pointed at the cab "—Mistress Quickly over there deserves a little of the blame?"

"I'm asking you to back off; you're married for Christ's sake."

Welles grabbed me by the collar. "You're asking *me* to back off, Junior? Well, here's my answer. Go fuck yourself. And I wouldn't worry your little heart about quitting—because you're fired. Effective this second. And you ever *mention* my wife again, I'll break your fucking neck. Now, you want to apologize to me, Junior? You want to go down on your knees and apologize for being a talentless little, meddling shit, then go right ahead."

I suddenly wanted to kill him—kill him for his ability to diminish people so completely. It was me. It was Sam Leve. It was Lloyd and Houseman. And, for once, I wanted to turn that destructiveness on him. And maybe, even more than that, I wanted to kill him because for the rest of his life he would be a star, and I would not.

I said, "You want to open your show tonight without a Lucius?"

"I'll cut your scene in two seconds."

"Then start cutting."

He used his fingers in a scissor gesture. "Done. You've got half an hour to get your stuff out of my theatre. One half hour, and if I see your talentless little face again, I'm calling the cops."

"Go to hell, you arrogant fuck."

"I hope you enjoyed your Broadway career, Junior, 'cause it's over."

He stepped into the taxi, slammed the door, and the cab pulled away.

I stood there shaking.

The city roared around me.

Eighteen

Vakhtangov met me on the stairs.

"I put your stuff in a box," he announced. "Orson told me to." He said nothing more and continued down the stairs.

A couple of extras were up in the dressing room playing hearts. They stopped talking when I entered. My gloves, my stage shoes, my overcoat, and my *John Gielgud's Hamlet* were inside an old carton.

They pretended not to notice me, but I heard somebody whisper: *"Sic transit gloria."* They all chuckled.

I didn't know whether to say goodbye or *screw you*. I said nothing.

Descending the stairs I met Cotten.

"Put that down," he said. "Don't you know Orson yet?"

I didn't say anything because I felt I might cry.

"My God, he pulls this every show," said Cotten. "He just wants you to kiss his ass—that's all. Then you laugh, and he laughs, and you both put this behind you. I was the goddamned star of *Horse Eats Hat*, and he fired me two hours before we opened just because I hammered Henrietta Kaye before he did." He laughed in his graceful, Virginia-gentleman way. "Just *apologize* to him, for Christ's sake."

"Apologize for what?"

"For whatever the hell he wants you to. You think it matters for what? Even *he* doesn't remember what this was about."

Lloyd was coming up the stairs. "You can't quit anyway. We still owe you five bucks—and we're not paying until we get *all* the details."

Cotten looked at him as if to say: *Do you believe I have to put up with this idiot?* "Apologize, Richard," he said.

"I can't. I don't have anything to apologize for."

"Apologize for giving Welles the clap," said Lloyd. "God, I hope you did. Can you imagine that son-of-a-bitch with the clap?" He threw himself into Brutus' funeral speech—stopping every few seconds to madly attack his groin. "'As Caesar loved me (*scratch, scratch*) I weep for him. As he was fortunate (*scratch, scratch*) I rejoice at it. As he was valiant I—(*two-fisted punching of groin*) Ooahhhh!'"

"Apologize," said Cotten.

"Let me think about it," I said.

"You don't have *time* to think about it."

"I finally stood up for myself. I finally *fought* for something. It's what you told me to do!"

"Holy Christ," said Lloyd. "You're taking advice

from *him*?"

Cotten said: "Let me talk to him for you."

"He told me I was a *talentless little shit*. Now I'm supposed to apologize to him?"

"I don't think *talentless little shit* is so bad," said Lloyd. "I mean, it's better than *unemployed* talentless little shit. Now *that's* bad."

"Will you shut up?" said Cotten.

"I'm explaining to him how the world works! Welles is the boss, so you tell him any goddamn crap he wants to hear. Who cares if you believe it? Kid, every boss in America is being told, 'Boss, that's a great idea. Boss, you're smart. I don't know how this place would be running without you,' and meantime every employee is really thinking: 'You stupid son-of-a-bitch, I hope you get run over by a truck, you dumb schmuck.'"

"Richard, I'm pleading with you," said Cotten. "Do it for me. I want you in the show. Orson's in his dressing room. He's expecting you."

I headed down the stairs unsure of what I was going to do.

In the second-floor dressing rooms a radio played Latin music. Then Evelyn Allen was on the stairs: her sneakers, her white short-sleeved T-shirt, bee-stung lips. In her hand was the rust-colored hardback book she was always reading.

"I was afraid you'd left already." She lowered her

eyes.

"I haven't quite disappeared completely yet."

"Richard, I wanted you to have this," she said, and she pressed the book into my hands. "I hope someday you might read it. And remember me."

"Thank you."

"I've got to get changed." She retreated into the dressing rooms.

I stood there a little bewildered.

The book was some ancient thing: *Monadology* by Gottfried Wilhelm von Leibniz. On the first blank page she'd written:

Nov. 11, 1937
Richard—I have no right to say this, but I love you. It's strange, but sometimes you feel connected to someone almost immediately. Please write to me, Richard, whatever happens. I hope we can possibly see each other in the future.
        love, E.

I read it over three times. *Holy Christ,* I thought. This woman hasn't said two words to me the entire show, and now she's telling me she's in love with me.

The world was feeling more and more like a madhouse.

Bryant Park. The leaves fell around me.

I looked down at my carton: my shoes, my *Caesar*

script, and *Monadology*. I read the inscription again. *Richard—I have no right to say this, but I love you.*

Oh, Evelyn, I thought. You're even more lost than I am.

I closed my eyes.

My neck and shoulder throbbed in tension.

I breathed slowly—tried to let the city pour into me.

I flipped through *Monadology*. I liked the inscription, crazy as it was. I read a sentence at random. *Every particle of matter in the universe experiences everything else in the universe, so much so that anyone who perceives accurately enough might read in any particle of matter what is happening everywhere, and even what has happened or will happen.... Thus every particle of matter can be perceived as a forest of living things, or a river of abundant fish.... There is nothing lifeless in the universe, no chaos, no disorder, though this may not be immediately clear to us.*"

This was the stuff Evelyn thought about? She was reading philosophy as she sat alone on the Mercury staircase? I read the passage a few more times. *There is nothing lifeless in the universe, no chaos, no disorder, though this may not be immediately clear to us.* She's standing onstage, enduring Joe Holland's paint-peeling breath, and she's thinking that there is nothing lifeless in the universe, no chaos, no disorder.

And if you believed that philosophy, didn't it mean you could never really do *anything* wrong? Never be out of grace? Even if you *wanted* to, there was no disorder possible....

So you trusted the universe?

I looked up into the trees.

Maybe there was nothing else to trust.

Then I thought for a moment about Orson Welles. And I thought about myself.

I took my billfold from my pocket and found the back of my driver's license where I'd filled out the change-of-information card. There, in my handwriting, it read Richard Orson Samuels.

I laughed at my own absurdity.

"Richard Kenneth Samuels," I said out loud.

Then I repeated my name.

Terrible, but mine.

Walking toward me, in a black overcoat, and smoking a cigar, was Orson Welles.

He laughed warmly. "Richard, old man, Joe said I might find you here." He shook my hand humbly, expansively. "What can I tell you? That I'm sorry? That we need you? Those words are paltry and inadequate to describe the depth of friendship that you and I share." He put his gloved hand on my shoulder, as if he were going to walk me toward Fifth, but I pulled away and faced him.

"Why don't you skip all the bunk about the depth of our friendship," I said, and for the first time I felt the power shifting to my side of the table. The son-of-a-bitch needed me.

"Whatever you say."

"All I wanted was to be treated as a human being—deserving of *some* dignity."

"It was never my intention to treat you any other way, Junior."

"Don't call me Junior."

"Sorry. I use the term affectionately."

"It diminishes me."

"Then no more." He gave me a Boy Scout salute. "Word of honor."

"Why do I want so much to believe you?"

Now we were walking down Fifth.

"Because you really *are* a God-created actor, Richard. Those weren't just words; you see, I recognized the look."

"The look?"

"The bone-deep understanding that your life is so utterly without meaning that simply to *survive* you have to reinvent yourself. Because if people can't *find* you, they can't dislike you. You see, if I can be Brutus for ninety minutes tonight—I mean, really *be* him from the inside out—then for ninety minutes I get this miraculous reprieve from being myself. That's what you see in every great actor's eyes, you know. You see someone weeping at the broken thing that he knows himself to be: that every gesture is affectation, that every stirring of the heart is instantly stuck dead into the performance book. And I don't mean to insult you with all this—I just sense it inside you, as it's inside me."

"I don't know what I feel anymore," I said. "In the last twenty-four hours I seem to have run the entire possible range of human emotions. I'm exhausted."

"Cigar? Cuban."

"Sure."

We stood on the steps of the library and I lit my cigar off his. We watched a businessman in an expensive-looking suit flirting with a much younger woman. He was offering her a cupful of hot chestnuts.

"Tonight I'm Brutus," said Welles. "And I want you to be Lucius." He touched my shoulder. "You may not like me, Richard—and, frankly, it's irrelevant to me whether or not you do. Our business together is to create the best art we can. That's all that matters. But I am asking you to give me this opening night. After tonight you can do whatever you want. But, Richard, give me this opening. I need you. Don't think about it; say *yes, Orson*. Say *yes, Orson*, right now."

"And Sam Leve gets his credit in the *Playbill* starting tomorrow?"

He looked at me sourly. "I've arranged that already."

"Promise it to me. He's my friend."

"I promise you. He'll get his credit."

"And you'll call my mother and tell her that I'm an important part of this show—and that it's urgent I miss some school?"

He smiled. "All right."

"And you'll call my principal and explain to him that all my absences are excused."

"All right."

"And the cast party tonight at Tony's? I want an invitation."

"Christ, you're underage!"

"Cover for me."

"Jesus, what an operator. All right, you can come to the cast party. Is there anything else you want? You want a position in the Roosevelt cabinet? Will you tell me we have a deal already?"

"Deal," I said.

We shook hands.

"And you better be brilliant," said Welles. "Because if you stink the whole deal is off!"

Nineteen

"Noel Coward, I believe, once said a hit smells like oysters," Coulouris announced loftily.

"Well, it certainly smells like fish in here," said Muriel. "My effing clothes stink from it. How do these look?" She flashed him her earrings.

A small notecard had been left for me backstage, and I opened it, imagining it might be a love letter from some stage-struck young woman whose heart had melted (*Oh, God!*) at my ukulele playing.

It was a white card with two hearts drawn on it. The hearts were joined by an arrow. Beneath the hearts was simply the signature: *Orson.*

Swell, I thought.

If it was meant as an apology, I accepted it.

The curtain went up at nine that night, but by eight you could feel the energy humming in the walls of the theatre: in the beams and the floorboards. The pure *noise* of it was thrilling. A sign outside the box office read: OPENS TONIGHT–SOLD OUT, but still people were standing on line, and the phones were ringing in the ticket office, and the phones were ringing in the projection room, and the phone backstage was flashing its "ring" light.

Welles had decided late that afternoon that he wanted still more music in the play, and as the well-wishers hurried out the stage door, he and Epstein continued to work out music cues.

"Now X means a fanfare."

"For Christ's sake, Orson, don't tell me X means a fanfare; if you want a fanfare then write the goddamn word 'fanfare' in the script. Why are we doing this forty minutes before curtain?"

An imposing-looking man pushed past me: tweed coat, Tartan scarf, curly black hair, rimless round eyeglasses.

"Clifford Odets!" said Welles. "Was this the face that launched a thousand hits!"

"Me? I'm just a tramp from Newark!" said Odets. "I think you know Luise." He gestured to a soulful-looking dark-haired starlet.

Luise pulled Odets's hand into Welles's. "Golden Boy, meet Wonder Boy."

Odets then gestured to a rumpled-looking man standing behind him, a man whose long graying hair stood out in massive disarray. "Orson, I'd like you to meet Dr. Albert Einstein."

"Honored," said Welles.

"I'm working with him to help the Jewish refugees in Europe."

Einstein curled his nostrils, "Is it my imagination or

does it smell from fish in here?" he said.

There was a shouting from upstage left, and somebody was yelling *You can't come in here!* and then an enormous Negro man in full African witch-doctor regalia, clutching a staff topped with a skull, came swooping across the stage.

"Meesta Whales! Meesta Whales!"

"Abdul!" shouted Orson. "You made it! Wonderful!" Welles hugged him. He turned to Einstein. "Abdul, this is Dr. Albert Einstein. You two probably have a lot in common; you're both doctors."

Houseman had come up from behind me. "Orson, Joe Holland says he can't go on, says he's having a heart attack. I think it's nerves, but I sent for an ambulance just in case. He's in your dressing room."

"This is just what I need."

A boy now edged himself onstage; he wore a white kitchen suit stenciled *Longchamps*. He held a covered silver tray. "Two steaks!" he called out. "One pineapple and a bottle of Scotch for Mr. Welles!"

"Junior, take that for me."

"*Richard,*" I said.

"I don't have time for this now. Did you tune the uke?"

I ran behind Welles carrying the tray as we headed through the remaining press people and the girlfriends. Welles turned to me. "Now let's see what the Christ *this* is about."

Holland was sitting in a chair in the center of Welles's dressing room. He was dressed in his Caesar uniform: green double-breasted military coat, brass buttons, black leather boots and gloves. He was breathing shallowly. The tiny hairs of his closely shaved face stood out against the unnatural paleness in his cheeks. "Can't do it, Orson; can't do it," he whispered between breaths. His eyes were open, and he was shaking his head *no*.

Roosevelt's voice came from the radio on the make-up table: *And so I place this wreath on the Tomb of the Unknown Soldier—*

"Shut that crap off," said Welles.

Evelyn Allen, now in her stage gown, sat holding Holland's gloved hand, rubbing his wrist. She wouldn't meet my eyes. George Duthie stood behind him massaging his shoulders. "Going to be fine, Joe. Perfectly fine. Just the old opening-night willies."

"Can't do it," said Holland. His voice cracked, and he turned his head away.

"Give him a shot of Scotch. Everybody outside," ordered Welles. "Look at me, Joe. *Look at me*. I want you to hear every word I say. Do you understand me?"

I lingered for a moment in the doorway. Welles had taken Holland's face in his hands, and he was forcing that face to meet his eyes. He spoke in his most commanding tones. "Listen, Joe. There are some actors who will study and practice and work their whole lives, and they'll be decent actors, and they'll get decent reviews. But there are other actors, Joe—listen to me—other actors whom I call *God-created*."

"Not me, Orson," whispered Holland. "Never me."

"Look at me," said Welles. "When I look in your eyes do you know what I see? I see *images of magnificence*."

I had heard enough. There was a boy about fourteen with blond hair standing outside the dressing room. "Mr. Welles told me to see him before the show. He said it was important."

The kid had *child actor* written all over his face. "He's busy, Junior," I said.

Madness seemed to be breaking loose everywhere I turned. In less than ten minutes the audience would be seated, and right now Lloyd stood center stage, and Jeannie Rosenthal was on a ladder focusing lights on him. Sam Leve was running around with a can of gray paint retouching his platforms.

"For God's sake, can *one* of our productions open on time," said Houseman, walking through the chaos. Then he was arguing with a man dressed in rubber boots and a fire hat.

"Let me see if I understand this," said the fire marshal. "The exit lights are going to be extinguished twice—"

"Positively not."

"I was told by that guy over there that—"

"He doesn't even work here," said Houseman. "He's a union agitator. A Communist! Do you honestly think the Mercury Theatre would endanger the life of even *one* member of our audience for a light cue? Can you imagine the liabilities we'd—"

"I was told that—"

"And I'm telling you there is no such thing. Have you even *seen* the show?"

"No, but—"

"Then what are we talking about?" said Houseman. He reached into his vest pocket. "Look, I want you to take two complimentary tickets for the show—in a purely professional capacity, of course."

"Gee, thanks."

Ash, the stage manager, ran out of the wings holding a telephone. "Is Sonja here? It's David O. Selznick!"

"Tell him I'm ready for my audition!" said Lloyd. Then he was parading along the stage doing a limp-wristed Southern belle. "Ah'll think of it all tomorrow at Tara. Tomorrow ah'll think of *some* way to get him back...."

"Will somebody find Sonja—and, people, *clear* the stage!" called Ash. "We're letting the audience in."

I ran up the stairs past the second floor: actors standing around dressed in military uniforms or dark overcoats. A radio playing. Somebody laughing.

This is it, I thought.

Evelyn passed me on the stairs. "I was looking for you," she said. She lowered her eyes. "I had no right to inscribe that book the way I did. I apologize."

"There's no need to—"

"But I felt from the beginning there was a connection between us. Have you ever read *The Great Chain of Being* by Arthur O. Lovejoy?"

Cotten was coming up the steps. "Get dressed, Richard. You going to Tony's later?"

"Welles said he might be able to sneak me in."

"Good." His predatory eye roved over Evelyn. "You're going, aren't you, Evey?"

"I don't like crowds very much."

"You *have* to go—and afterwards, there's this *exquisite* little place I want to show you in the Village. Marta. No crowds, just writers, artists. *Exactly* the kind of place you'd love."

"Isn't that the place where they've got that special on the menu?" I asked. "What's it called again? 'Quadruple Something'?"

"That's the place!" said Cotten—and he was already heading upstairs with his arm on Evelyn's shoulder.

From a radio somewhere I could hear Rudy Vallee singing "Have You Met Miss Jones?" I thought: *This is the song that's going to pin this day inside me forever.*

Up in the third-floor dressing room I did stretching exercises. That dressing room—its stink of cigarettes, its signatures on the wall, its water stains—it was somehow all exactly right.

Hoysradt was checking the cleanliness of his teeth in the mirror.

I put on my military shirt and pants.

"Five minutes!" somebody shouted up from the stairs.

I brushed my hair. "How do I look?" I asked.

"Horrible," said Hoysradt.

Cotten and Lloyd were standing in the wings. Coulouris was rubbing lotion into his hands, and the noise of the audience was still rising—the sound of two balconies and an orchestra.

I went back upstairs to check my hair and my fly for the ten-thousandth time, and I stopped on the landing to open a window. A police siren rolled through a nearby street, indifferent to the affairs of the Mercury Theatre. I headed down the stairs for the last time, holding tight to the bannister. All right, I said to myself, if I don't fall down these stairs, then I'm opening in *Caesar*....

There was, of course, no curtain, but if you stood behind the thunderdrum you could still remain unseen and *just* see the edge of the audience. They murmured and stood in the aisles and checked their ticket stubs and

planned where they'd go for drinks after the show.
Ninety minutes out of their lives—half of them would
probably forget it by the time they hit the street. But
there were also the critics. Their names sounded on your
tongue like a roll call of Princeton professors: Brooks
Atkinson, Granville Vernon, Heywood Broun, Stark
Young, Joseph Wood Krutch.

Welles stood by the fire extinguisher giving Holland
a last-minute pep-talk. Then he took the phone off the
lightboard and dialed two numbers. "Augusta? Welles.
Anybody shows up late *hold them* 'til the blackout before
the conspirators' scene. Is that understood? Those back
doors do not open for Jesus Christ himself." He replaced
the phone, and whispered to the stage manager. "That's
all I need, some *putz* from Brooklyn coming in late with
his six consumptive aunts. How many 'friends' in the
balcony?"

"About forty."

He said. "All right, let's rip their throats out.
Jeannie, pull the lights." He rubbed his hands nervously.
"This is the night," he recited, *"that either makes me or
fordoes me quite."*

Jeannie nodded to the union guy working the
lightboard, and one by one the old iron dimmers were
pulled. You heard waves of *shhhh* as the rows of
houselights were extinguished.

Then near-silence out there. Silence on stage.

Welles whispered to the musicians behind him. "Loud,
fellas. Wake up the sons-of-bitches." He turned to
Jeannie. "All right, are we ready? Black it out.
Showtime!"

There was the clunk of the master dimmer, and in
one second every light in the entire theatre—including
the exit signs—fell into complete darkness. Only one
tiny bulb with the power of a flashlight burned atop the
lightboard. Welles continued to whisper—urgent now.
"Hold the music 'til I cue you. Four beats." He took a
slow count. "—three—two—one...make 'em
sweat...and...." He raised his right arm like a
conductor—then gently caressed in the downbeat:
"...music."

The horns and the organ and the drum blared their
military-sounding march. Then Welles, without looking
behind him, raised his right arm again—held it until he
heard an exact moment he knew in the score, and then
gracefully let it fall. "...and lights."

I smiled, thinking of what the audience must be
feeling: seeing this dark spectacle for the first time—this
Caesar without a toga in sight.

Total blackness. Then the music, crescendoing
now—suddenly cut.

From a mile out there, way at the back of the house
came Duthie's cry: *Caesar!*

Backlit onstage, Holland and his soldiers stood in

silhouettes of menace—gunbelts, epaulets—and Holland was shouting over the heads of the audience, his gaze somewhere toward the back: "'Peace! Bid every noise be still!'"

That cry again. *Caesar!* Duthie in his overcoat now climbing the steps to the stage.

"'Who is it in the throng that calls on me?'" demanded Holland. "'Marc Antony?'"

Coulouris snapped to attention: "'Caesar, my lord?'"

And we were off and running!

Welles entered in his pinstriped suit. Modest applause.

The thunderdrum was struck and thrummed with two padded hammers—and its thunder kept rolling softly as Gabel, in uniform, entered by the upstage ramp into a pool of light. Outlined against the blood-red wall, Gabel looked like some demon of war.

"'Will you go see the order of the course?'" he asked.

Welles was startled at the voice. "'...Into what dangers, Cassius, would you lead me....'" Welles sat down on the front step; it was Welles's first moment to let the audience really *see* him—without elaborate makeup, up close and looking magnificently like a star. He played it with a deliciously self-indulgent slowness, as if he weren't reciting the words of some dusty play, but as if he'd just thought of those words this moment—pulled them hesitantly out of the air to give shape to his confused mind. "'But wherefore do you hold me here so long? What is it that you would impart to me?'"

And so the scene went with Gabel getting most of the lines—but Welles was the one you watched. You didn't listen to Gabel's speech so much as you watched Welles react to it. "'The fault, dear Brutus, lies not in our stars, but in ourselves, that we are underlings,'" said Gabel—and Welles turned to meet his eyes.

I thought, Oh, you've got them where you want them, Wonder Boy.

More military music, perfectly cued this time, and the soldiers fell silent as Holland and Coulouris and Joe Cotten marched by.

Holland: "'Yond Cassius has a lean and hungry look. He thinks too much—such men are dangerous....'"

There was nothing in Holland's delivery that suggested his breakdown fifteen minutes earlier.

Then there were stabs of lightning onstage. The thunderdrum boomed in your chest, and Epstein held a bass note on the organ that rumbled the whole theatre.

The storm was up.

Linking scenes, faster now—flashlights, men in their overcoats and their working-class shoes—and that drumming of those footsteps in the darkness.

A few latecomers were seated. Welles had been right about that, too—hold them for the first fifteen minutes until the mood had been set.

Was he ever wrong?

Now the worklight filtered through the hanging apparatus of the lights—and the stage was filled with sinister shadows.

Muriel Brassler stood next to me in the wings waiting for her one scene. She held a small mirror before her, and she fluffed her hair behind her ears to let her silver earrings show more clearly. Then she placed a tiny diamond ring on her left hand. She checked her nose hair, then asked me to hold her mirror while she stepped back to admire the full effect. She caught her reflection—threw back her shoulders, and it was as if she were melting into another person in front of my eyes. Gone was the abrasiveness, and before me, instantly, stood noble Portia. "'Brutus, my lord,'" she called—and she strode center stage.

If Welles was angry about her jewelry he didn't show it. He held her hand, and he played the scene with enormous tenderness.

"You can tell they've screwed," said Lloyd over my shoulder.

The lightning flashed and her scene was over. She whispered as she exited. "Goddamnit, I *begged* him not to stand on the same step with me." There were tears in her eyes.

"You were great," I said.

"Was I?" she asked.

"You're what I call a *God-created actress*," I said with perfect seriousness.

"I love you," she said and kissed me.

I performed my three lines about Cassius showing up at the door, and I played them so fast I didn't have time to be nervous. *Too fast*, I thought as I exited. *Play it like Welles, Richard*—give the audience the chance to *like* the character you're playing.

Then I was down in the trap with Grover Burgess and his crutch. We were both waiting for our cues.

"Nervous?" he whispered.

"Only if people ask me if I'm nervous."

"Nervous?"

I checked my fly yet again. I didn't actually feel nervous so much as I just wanted to get out there, grab the thing by the throat, and be doing it.

Then Burgess was giving me a little push. I climbed the ladder and was walking downstage into the light.

And from out of that dark, silent audience I distinctly heard two voices loudly cough out, "Black Crow!"

Oh, Christ. I bit my lip. I instantly lost my concentration. Welles was staring at me, waiting for my line. He gave me an almost imperceptible nod.

"*Here*," I said and pointed, "is a sick man that would speak with you." I exited downstage in a haze. My feet tingling, chest hammering; I was sweating.

One line and I almost blew it!

The play went raging on.

I sat down behind the thunderdrum. *Focus! Focus! Calm down, you idiot!*

So Stefan and Skelly had shown up—the crazy sons-of-bitches!

I laughed. *You're not going to mess up, Richard. I look in your eyes, and you know what I see? Images of magnificence!* And if I was going to throw up with nervousness, then nervousness was part of the great chain of being! *There is nothing lifeless in the universe, no chaos, no disorder, though this may not be immediately clear to us.* Yeah!

You actually heard a member of the audience cry out when the first knife came out of Sherman's pocket.

Then one by one they stabbed Caesar—all the music ended, the thunder ceased—just those banks of hard-white lights burning into the audience's eyes, and Joe Holland tumbling down the line of assassins 'til at last he faced Welles. Half-dead, he gripped Welles's coat. Welles met his eyes with a look of compassion—and you wondered for a second if he was actually going to stab him.

"'*Et tu, Brute?* Then fall Caesar,'" gasped Holland, and he fell against Welles's knife in a dying embrace, the bladder bag of red dye staining his uniform.

From that point the narrative drive of the play was

unstoppable. The air was charged, racing along like some crazy Warner Brothers thriller.

Welles did "Romans, countrymen, and lovers" at the foot of the downstage platform. I smelled hot oil, and I turned to see Ash pumping an atomizer on a smoke machine. As the smoke drifted out to the stage it caught the beams of light in stark, angular planes of shadow.

"Swell effect!" I whispered to Ash. He was dressed in a black overcoat because he was also an extra in the Cinna scene.

"Orson thought of it a half hour ago," he whispered, shaking his head. "Did you ever try to find a smoke machine in half an hour?"

A *chung* from the dimmer board and the lamps hidden under the stage shot their beams straight up into the smoke.

The audience gasped. Some people in the balcony applauded. Then Coulouris was up on the velvet-covered pulpit, and around him rose the columns of light.

Now the crowd of extras (including Ash) had rushed out and were jostling, shouting below him to hear Caesar's will.

Welles told me to continue pumping the atomizer to maintain the smoke effect.

Coulouris was playing the crowd with everything he had. "'Have patience, gentle friends, I must not read it....

It will inflame you. It will make you mad!'"

Still they chanted and stomped: *The will! Read us the will!*

Coulouris raised his gloved hand into the smoke-filled light. "'You will *compel* me then to read the will?'"

They pulled away as he descended from the pulpit, and then they joined him around the blanket-covered coffin of Caesar.

Coulouris's voice became tender and nostalgic. "'You all do know this mantle....I remember the first time ever Caesar put it on....'"

Then he yanked the blanket away, and they were screaming at the sight of his blood-smeared corpse.

Lights poured sideways from the wings, and the figures in black ran among the beams shouting: *Revenge! Revenge!*

Then, in one second, like a cut in a film, the stage turned cold and empty. The smoke dissipated, and just that solitary bulb burned at the top of the back wall.

Welles had been right about that, too. The effect was the perfect evocation of a deserted alley.

I wondered how somebody twenty-two years old could be so unerringly right. Maybe he *was* some kind of genius.

And just when the audience thought all the tension and terror they could bear had been wrung out of them, Lloyd walked out alone into that deserted alley with a sheaf of poems in his hand.

> *"I dreamt tonight that I did feast with Caesar,*
> *And things unluckily charge my fantasy…"*

Then from out of the street shadows came the men in the slouch hats—hands in their pockets, cruelty in their voices:
"'What is your name?'"
"'Whither are you going?'"
"'Where do you dwell?'"
And Lloyd had his hands raised above his head, tripping over his legs, backing up to the brick wall, dropping his poems—shouting now: "'*I'm Cinna—Cinna the poet!*'"

Epstein hit the horror chord, and he opened the pedal as loud as it could go.

Blackness and military drums—and the audience got a chance to breathe just a little during the quiet tent scene between Welles and Gabel.

I stood in the wings and checked the tuning of the uke. The trumpet player watched me. "Nervous?" he asked.

"Only if people ask me if I'm nervous."

"Nervous?"

Brutus and Cassius were apologizing to each other before the battle that would kill them both.

They shook hands. "'O my dear brother,'" said Gabel. "'This was an ill beginning of the night. Never come such division 'tween our souls. Let it not, Brutus.'"

Three lines and I'm on.

Three lines and I'm singing in front of Joseph Wood Krutch and Stark Young—can't think of it—

"'Lucius!'" Welles called.

Oh, Jesus.

"'Here, my good Lord.'"

Voice didn't crack.

"'What, thou speak'st drowsily? Poor knave, I blame thee not, thou art o'erwatched.'"

Then came a cannon-blast coughing from the audience, and barely hidden in the hacking phlegm was a voice nearly shouting out: "Black Crow!"

Oh, shut up, I prayed. Please, God, shut up!

"'Lucius,'" said Welles. "'Here's the book I sought for so.'"

"'I was sure your lordship did not give it me.'"

Now a wild, cartoon-like sneeze from the audience, and somewhere in that sneeze I heard: "Black Crow!"

At this point I didn't even know what I was speaking. I was just pronouncing syllables.

Don't laugh, Richard. Just don't laugh.

"'I should not urge thy duty past thy might,'" said Welles. Then his voice softened. "'I know young bloods look for a time of rest.'"

I looked into Welles's brown eyes, and I was really *listening* to him.

And my voice grew more tender. "'I have slept, my lord, already,'" I said, and I smiled at Welles as one might smile at his father.

Welles looked at me for a second, then tousled my hair affectionately. It was a complete surprise—a gesture he had never done before. "'It was well done,'" he smiled, "'and thou shalt sleep again. I will not hold thee long. If I do live, I will be good to thee....'" His voice broke in sadness.

I sat on the stage and sang my song. I fixed my eyes on a lamp attached to the first balcony, and I emptied my head of everything else.

Orpheus with his lute,
Made trees and the mountaintops that freeze,
Bow themselves when he did sing...

Then the lights faded to absolute blackness, and my part in *Julius Caesar* was over.

Twenty

The lights streamed upward from the floor; it was the last line of the play. Coulouris stood over the body of Welles. "'His life was gentle,'" Coulouris said, "'and the elements so mixed in him that Nature might stand up and say to all the world, *This was a man!*'"

The military music rose as the soldiers stood there without moving.

Then total blackness.

Silence.

Then they didn't applaud; they *roared*.

The noise broke over every side; it rolled to the stage from the first balcony, from the second balcony, and it didn't stop.

The place was thundering. It was a hurricane of sound.

"My God," said Epstein.

Jeannie Rosenthal stood by the lightboard, arms folded, face flushed with pleasure.

You could feel it in the floorboards. The torrent of noise rising until your eyes watered in gratitude. And, even at that moment, I knew it was the tidal wave of approval that you heard just once in your life.

Welles, breathless, soaked, took a gulp of pineapple juice. He wiped his forehead. "Start the curtain-call music," he ordered. He looked around at Coulouris, then at me. He hugged me. "We did it!" Across the stage I could see Gabel embracing Joe Holland; Lloyd was punching Cotten, grinning. Welles gulped another mouthful of pineapple juice, then began laughing, almost spitting it out. "How the hell do I top this!"

The applause didn't stop for three curtain calls. Finally Welles came on alone, and the entire audience stood up. Even the cast members and the technicians came out and applauded him. He bowed five times—each time more deeply and more slowly. "He's worse than Jack Barrymore," Coulouris said.

Flowers arrived, and Houseman was beaming, face rose-colored, shaking hands, and the audience wasn't *leaving*. There were telegrams, and more flowers, and there was Sonja suddenly in a green velvet strapless evening gown, an orchid in her hair. She stood in the wings laughing and hugging everybody. When I hugged her she said, "You were brilliant, Richard."

There were flashbulbs, and the stage streamed with people. Abdul, in his African headdress, strode up the aisle. "Beeg heet!" he cried out to Houseman.

Two of Orson's old theatre buddies from Ireland

introduced themselves to me. They were *extravagantly* effeminate, and had their hands all over me as they talked. "I think this boy would make a *priceless* Hamlet, don't you, Hill?"

"With us behind him...."

Then somebody was shouting: "Black Crow! Black Crow!" and those two drunken lunatics Skelly and Stefan, in their jackets and ties, were pumping my hand. "You stunk," said Stefan, "but that girl in the tight dress? You could see her nipples."

"Thanks for coming, you crazy assholes."

"Is she not wearing a bra or something?"

Skelly said, "Wait 'til the broads at school find out you're in a Broadway show. You'll be slamming before Saturday!"

"You need a ride home? We got Drift's old man's Chevy."

"I'm going to the cast party."

"Can we come? Is that girl going to be there?"

Lloyd was walking around shaking hands. "I was magnificent, wasn't I?" he kept repeating. "Wasn't I something else? Did you ever see an audience react like that?"

Cotten had about ten girls around him, giggling, flirting.

Coulouris was leaning against the brick wall holding forth to a group of friends. He sipped from a glass of champagne. "I knew the show was destined for greatness from the first rehearsal," he recalled. "I remember seeing with a startling clarity that the role of Marc Antony was the psychological *centerpiece* of the play. And that's when it all came together."

"I've never heard the funeral oration performed like that," said one of his friends.

Coulouris nodded. "My staging as well."

"Brilliant."

Epstein was playing "Lullaby of Broadway" on the organ. The horn player was trying to improvise around him.

Evelyn Allen, in her purple gown, stood talking to some guy with a big gut and black mustache. She held a bouquet of roses. She saw me approaching and her voice got soft.

"Evelyn," I said. "You were wonderful."

"Thank you."

"Lovely, sensitive—"

"Oh, don't embarrass me," she said.

The guy with the gut was watching me suspiciously now. "You will excuse me," he said. He had a fairly thick German accent. "But do I know you?"

"He's in the play, Christoph."

"Oh, yes. I'm so sorry. So pleased to meet you," he said. He extended his hand.

Evelyn lowered her voice. "Richard, this is my

husband."

He shook my hand as if his entire manhood depended upon it.

"Swell to meet you," I said. "Evelyn, I'll talk to you later, O.K.?"

Ahhhh! Get me outta here!

I practically ran right into Muriel, who had changed into a scarlet gown with a matching hat. She was wearing fresh lipstick, and she was flirting with some roly-poly guy who looked about sixty. "Orson and I are so *simpatico*, I guess," she explained. "I suppose I just like working with *men*, you know? I could never do a play like *The Women*—forty characters, all women. My God, I'd go out of my mind. No, I need to be around men."

The little guy nodded appreciatively.

The band was playing, and some people were trying to dance, but there wasn't any room. Most people were heading out for the party.

Sam Leve came up to me with the *Playbill* and shook his head. "Tomorrow I get my credit," he said. "But tomorrow the critics don't come."

"Everybody here knows all the work you did," I said.

"Yeah, but everybody here don't count."

I hit the dressing room stairs at a run to change into my street clothes, but Cotten stopped me on the second-floor landing. He was looking glum. There was an open window, and I could hear a light rain dripping on the fire escape.

"What's eating you, Fertilizer?" I asked. I took a swig from my root beer bottle. "Jeez, I thought I was going to forget the whole lyric. You know, until I actually *sang* the words, until they actually came from my mouth, I had no idea I still remembered them. You taking a cab to the party? Maybe we can share. How was I? Brilliant, wasn't I? That's what I am. A brilliant young man. I'm thinking of forming my own theatrical company with me as the director and the star. You want to be in it? You can take some of the smaller roles." I did my Gabriel Heatter impersonation: "There's *good* news tonight!"

"Not so good news. You don't know yet?"

"What?"

"Orson hasn't told you yet?"

"Told me what?"

"You're fired, Richard."

I stood staring at him. "I'm *what?*"

I could still hear the rain falling on the fire escape.

"I'm sorry to be the one to tell you. Orson's not only a son-of-a-bitch, he's a coward."

"Joe, you're kidding—"

"He never forgave you; he just wanted his opening night."

The root beer bottle slipped from my hand and spilled on the floor. "Tell me you're kidding me, Joe. Because this isn't funny."

"Sonja told me. Did you see that blond kid hanging around the stage tonight?"

"Yeah," I said, and I felt something large and sad rising in my throat. I tried to mop up the soda with my shoe.

"He's your replacement."

"What's the gag?"

"He's been *hired* already."

"Joe, stop kidding me."

"Sonja wanted me to break the news to you, to tell you how *absolutely terrible* she feels. Though not absolutely terrible enough to tell you herself."

Down below, the band was still playing.

"Joe, this can't be happening. The show's a hit. *I'm* a hit."

"Orson apparently gave the kid the script, told him to learn his lines by tomorrow."

"*Tomorrow?* Joe—he can't learn the part by tomorrow."

"Richard, I'm sorry. Orson's going to give you all this crap that it's Actor's Equity, and that the kid's an Equity Junior Member, which he is—but that's horseshit—it's not about Equity....Orson is a sick man in many ways; a dark, sick man. I tried to talk to him. He won't even *listen* to me. No. Made up his mind. Can't be budged."

"It is *not* going to end like this, all right? I refuse to allow that possibility. I'm fighting this. I mean, what the hell did I do wrong? I didn't do one thing. I've been to every rehearsal. The show's a hit—I'm—"

"Don't you get it? Orson can't be wrong."

"I said *one* thing, Joe. I said Sonja was my lov—my girlfriend. I fought for her—just like you told me to!"

"Maybe that was lousy advice."

"I said that he should back off. That's *all* I said."

"You told him that?"

"Yeah, well, I started to—right before he tore my head off, but he *apologized* to me, Joe—he said—"

Cotten shook his head. "And you took Leve's side when Orson pulled his credit?"

"What was I supposed to do? Let him call that man a credit-stealing Jew and not say one word? Is that what everybody *does* around here? Jesus Christ!" I kicked the wall. "O.K., what do I do, Joe? Tell me what I have to do. Am I supposed to apologize to him? 'Cause if that's what it takes to get my part back, I'll do it. I'll do whatever—"

"I don't think it'll help. I'm sorry."

"He gave me *this*." From my pocket I took out the small white card with two hearts drawn on it. "Doesn't this mean anything?"

Cotten shook his head, reached into his shirt pocket, and pulled out the same card. "He gave everybody the same bullshit."

"Well, I don't care what it means, 'cause I *refuse* to accept that this is over. It's not over—O.K.? I refuse to accept that he can make some five-second decision because he's in a shitty mood, and that's it—that my career in the Mercury Theatre is over. Is he here? I'm talking to him right now!" I moved down the stairs. "*I'm not accepting this.*"

Cotten grabbed me. "He never wanted to bring you back, Richard; don't you get it? He wanted his opening night."

"So I stand up *once*, and that's it? That's the end of my job here? That's not fair, Joe. It was *one* time."

"Richard, my heart goes out to you—you've been treated like shit. I don't know what to tell you. I'm going to the party; I'll *try* to talk to him. But don't expect any—"

"No, *I'm* going to the party."

I ran down the stairs—furious—ready to argue my part back with Welles. The words I'd say were flying through my head. *This is not fair, and there is not one person in this company who would agree with—*

Cotten called down after me. "Don't! Richard, you're going to make it worse. Let me—"

Vakhtangov was standing guard by Welles's dressing room. "He's gone. They're all gone."

"Oh, fuck you." I tried the door. It was locked.

I tore back up the stairs to get my hat and coat. Cotten was dressed and ready to leave.

"Wait for me!"

"Richard! For Christ's sake! Listen to me! He won't back down tonight. I'm telling you; don't go to the party! You will only make it worse."

I stopped running. "He can't *dismiss* people like this! People's lives just don't exist on the whim of Orson Welles! Don't I count, Joe? Don't I count at all?"

He looked at me with compassion.

"You mean to tell me that no one in this company would stand up for me? Would argue for me?"

"You're asking them to walk away from a hit show for you? In the middle of a Depression?"

I opened my mouth, but there were no more words.

"*I'll* argue for you, Richard. That's all I can do."

"If I were there—in front of people—at the party—"

"So Welles is going to back down in front of the whole company? With you standing there? That's what you're expecting?"

I held my head. "I don't know what I'm expecting."

"Go home, Richard."

"*This is home!*"

The theatre was nearly empty. I stood by the open third-floor window. The air felt rainy.

Next to the window, outside, a ladder led up to the roof. I wiped my eyes and stepped onto the fire escape.

Stefan and Skelly had gone home. Everyone had gone home.

I climbed the ladder.

On the roof, New York was lit like an enormous stage set: a thicket of supporting cables, ventilator shafts, streetlights—all silhouetted in the fog. It reminded me of the night I'd slept with Sonja.

I sat on a tar-paper-covered abutment. Its wetness soaked through my pants. The rain was a fine mist now.

In my head I still argued my part back from Welles.

Maybe tomorrow he'd listen....

I removed my hat and rubbed my temples. Then I took my scarf and tied it as tightly as I could, like a headband, around my forehead. It seemed to ease the ache that was spreading behind my eyes.

My ears rang with *Caesar.*

Poor knave, I blame thee not,

Thou art o'erwatched.

This is how it ends, I thought. And there you are, unsure of everything but your own headache—tumbling back to some old sense of belonging nowhere.

I tried to shake the self-pity, but I felt as if I were growing physically smaller.

And I said to myself: This is too small a loss to feel this kind of despair, Richard. You haven't made the theatre your life. This has been just one lucky week for you—one week that came and sparkled and passed.

And still part of me argued with Welles. It pleaded: *What did I do that was so wrong?*

Maybe I could call Tony's—say I was somebody else—
maybe he'd get the phone—or I'd just show up there and
force my way in and—

I walked to the edge of the roof and looked out over
the city—its immensity in the night. The buildings rose
like the massive hulls of ships. A fire engine howled
below. A bus passed. And the illuminated headlines
wrapped around the Times Building. And the rain fell on
every brick and stone of the city.

From my pocket I took out the small card Welles had
given me. Two hearts joined by an arrow. *Orson.*

"Kiss my ass, Orson Welles," I said, and flicked the
card over the side of the roof.

I heard myself breathing, and I watched my breath
steam into the fog. The tension in my neck was
loosening a little.

I walked along the edge of the roof. I studied the city
rising in its towers and wires—and I thought: *What if I*
closed my eyes? What if I counted to five, and then opened
my eyes again, and the whole city would be made perfect—
and everything under the face of God would be exactly where
it was supposed to be, and everyone would be doing exactly
what he was supposed to be doing, and every speck of dust
would be exactly in its right place? I shut my eyes and
imagined the world turning to such a paradise, and I
counted to five—and I opened my eyes and saw the city
exactly as it had been before. Unaltered. Traffic passed.

Somewhere below a neon light blinked.

And I thought: Could this *be* paradise? Maybe every particle of dust *is* exactly where it's supposed to be. Every turning, every heartache, every atom—exactly where it's supposed to be—exactly where it could only be? *There is nothing lifeless in the universe, no chaos, no disorder, though this may not be immediately clear to us.* If only I could believe that. And the darkness and the skyscrapers and the fog and every water droplet—a kind of life: complex, connected—a kind of paradise, at least the only kind of paradise I would ever know. This crazy, beautiful web of light and stone.

Footsteps on the roof; it was Sonja in her raincoat. "Richard, I'm sorry," she began. "Orson is intractable. Do you believe me that I tried? I gave it everything I had...."

I was still thinking about paradise.

"Richard?"

"Oh, I believe you," I said.

"Orson's playing the Tyrannical Director again. I'm sorry. I tried to talk to him. Joe Cotten tried to talk to him. John tried. Maybe in a day or two he'll change his mind. What am I saying? He's not going to change his mind." She stood there, a silhouette with her hands in her pockets.

"Sonja, what did I do that was so wrong?"

"You told the boss the truth."

"And what are you supposed to tell the boss?"

"'You're great, boss.'"

"That's it?"

"That's it."

"So everybody lies...."

"I'm sorry, Richard."

"Can you arrange it so I can talk to him for five minutes? That's all I want. O.K.? He doesn't have to change his mind. I just want five minutes."

She had nothing to say—and even as I'd asked the question, its meaninglessness pained me.

"You know," I said, "a couple of days ago I was thinking that it would be the greatest thing in the world to be Orson Welles—to think like him, see the world through his eyes. You know, to have that static charge you were talking about? But I was just thinking: even if I was exactly like Orson Welles, even if I woke up tomorrow with all his talents, an exact copy of Orson Welles—who would I be? I'd be the guy-who-sounds-like-Orson-Welles. Wouldn't I? I'd be the guy-who-directs-like-Orson Welles. I'd be the world's greatest Orson Welles impersonator. And I would *always* be that. Always the second-rate Orson Welles."

"Whoever said you had to be Orson Welles?"

"I did. I mean, I want to accomplish things, you know? As much as you do. I'm filled with dreams, too. Art. Music. Theatre. Enormous, absurd dreams."

"So who's stopping you?"

"What I mean is, I can never be a first-rate Orson Welles. Do you know what I'm saying? That job is already taken. I seem to be the last person on earth who's figured this out. I'm Richard Kenneth Samuels. God, what a lousy name. *But that's who I am.* Nothing more or less. Does any of this make sense to you?"

"Not really," she said gently.

"It's just something I'm feeling...," I said. "You going to the party?"

She checked her watch. "My date's picking me up downstairs. He told me he was going to be late."

"Not Welles, Sonja. At least tell me it's not Welles."

"It's David O. Selznick."

"You're going to the party with David O. Selznick?" She nodded.

"You're amazing."

"You want to hear my prediction?" she said. "I'll be working for him within two weeks, and within two months I'll be a production assistant on *Gone with the Wind.* And can I make a little prediction about you?"

"Right now I couldn't handle a bad one."

"It's a good one. Possibly a great one. It's that you're not an actor, Richard. You're a writer. I told you that before. You're an observer. That's your gift. Look at you, Richard—you sit and you take it all in."

"I don't want to be an observer."

"But that's who you are. Actors need to be loved,

Richard. You don't need to be loved like that."

"...and what do production assistants need?"

"Power," she said. "They need to be in a position where no one can ever relegate them to insignificance. Or dismiss them. Not ever. And that's who I am."

"I want so much to be angry with you, Sonja—but when you're actually here it all seems to dissolve away. I wish you luck, I guess."

"I won't need luck. I don't believe in luck."

I looked out at the city. "I don't think I believe in luck anymore either," I said. "It's kind of a relief not to believe in luck, isn't it? But I think I believe in something...I don't know if I could even articulate what it is. The improbable beauty of the world?"

"Of *this* world?"

"Even this world," I said. *"Though this may not be immediately clear to us."*

She shrugged, uncomprehendingly. "Well, you've got an interesting belief. Whatever it means." She adjusted her collar. "But, hey, I don't want to keep Mr. Selznick waiting, do I? How do I look?"

"Like a girl who's going to give one blindingly beautiful parting kiss to her *cavaliere*."

She walked over and gave me a light kiss on the side of my head.

"Your hair smells like black licorice," I said.

I thought about showing up at the party.

I didn't.

I just didn't have the stomach to fight anymore that night.

Maybe I'd call the theatre tomorrow. Maybe with time he'd change his—

I walked toward Penn Station through the fog, and New York looked like a painting. Perfect and inexpressibly fragile. And even Orson Welles couldn't take that away from me.

"Sherlock Holmes weather!" somebody in a doorway announced as I passed Macy's. Then I stood for a moment and tried to force myself to remember the streetlight and the mist and the adhesive sound of the tires on the wet street. And I thought: *Someday I'll use all this.*

Friday, November 12
Twenty-One

I woke from a restless sleep filled with dreams of a party: Orson Welles standing behind a circular bar, and one by one he pointed a finger at his friends to join him in the center. They were all laughing and celebrating, and still I waited for him to point to me.

The room was airless, and I felt a headache smeared across the left side of my face.

It was five-thirty in the morning. I switched on the lamp and looked at my *Playbill* from last night—a simple white cover with

THE MERCURY THEATRE

printed in the center in dark brown.

There on the inside under the "Call for Philip Morris" boy it read:

LUCIUS...........PLAYED BY...........RICHARD SAMUELS

I touched my name with my finger.

Who's Who in the Cast. Orson Welles (Brutus) was

born in Kenosha, Wisconsin and came to the American
theatre by way of Dublin, Ireland. In this country he has
played Marchbanks with Katharine Cornell, and Mercutio
and Tybalt in her production of "Romeo and Juliet." Last
season he played the title part of his own production of
"Doctor Faustus." He also has directed the Negro
"Macbeth," and has directed and appeared in such programs
on the radio as—

I tossed the *Playbill* on the floor.

I sat in the back of Dr. Mewling's Shakespeare class.
Kristina Stakuna arrived late. She was dressed in her
blue-and-white cheerleading uniform. I smiled at her—
just Richard: the old friend who talked to her yesterday
when she stole a smoke under the pine trees. Today she
didn't even see me.

"Now where were we?" Mewling sat down and took
the paper clip off his sheaf of yellow legal paper. "Now
don't all overwhelm me. Where were we? We were
talking about Shakespeare's chief source for *Julius
Caesar*, which was—don't all shout it at once now—
Plutarch's *Lives*, that's correct. Sir Thomas North's
translation of Plutarch's *Lives*."

I stared out the window in misery. It was really
getting to be winter out there. The trees in the courtyard
were black etchings against a wash of gray.

And I suddenly realized how tired I was. So much

had happened—the train rides, the rehearsals, the arguments, Joe Cotten on the stairs telling me I was fired, Sonja in her raincoat on the roof. My arms ached. My feet hurt. I wondered how anybody could keep up that pace? Who could live like that—day after day?

Orson Welles could.

Mewling placed a page of his notes on the bottom of the pile and continued talking to himself. "Perhaps if I read an extract from Sir Thomas North's translation of Plutarch's *Lives* aloud it will make this all clear. Plutarch writes that, quote, when it was told to him that Antony and Dolabella were in a plot against him, he said he did not fear such fat, luxurious men, but rather pale, lean fellows, meaning Cassius and Brutus, unquote. Now does this Plutarchian passage parallel any important *lines* in the text we were discussing yesterday? Come on, not everybody at once; we discussed this yesterday. Not *one* single person in this class can tell me the lines which parallel that passage? It occurs in act one, scene two; take out your books, ladies and gentlemen. Act one, scene two. We read this yesterday. Mr. Samuels, do you really expect to find the answer out the window?"

"It parallels Caesar's speech to Antony," I said without taking my eyes from the window, "which goes: 'Yond Cassius has a lean and hungry look. He thinks too much, such men are dangerous.'"

"Excellent," said Mewling.

I could hear Joe Holland's voice perfectly in my ear, and I went on reciting. "'He is a great observer, and he looks quite through the deeds of men. He loves no plays as thou dost, Antony; he hears no music. Seldom he smiles and smiles in such a sort as if he mocked himself and scorned his spirit that could be moved to smile at anything.'"

"Impressive," said Mewling.

And still I went on. "'Such men as he are never at heart's ease whiles they behold a greater than themselves, and therefore are they very dangerous.'"

"May I ask how you know the text so well?" asked Mewling.

I looked at him. "I was in the play once."

"Oh, *really?* And when was that?"

"Last night."

Caroline was now sitting at the Black Crow lunch table. She and Stefan weren't even hiding anything now. I sat at the far end of the table, and I listened.

The final performance of *Growing Pains* was taking place that night in the auditorium. Caroline was excited; everybody was talking about the huge party they were going to have afterwards at Kristina Stakuna's.

Then Stefan tried to pull me in by telling everybody at the table that he and Skelly had seen me on Broadway last night—but before he could even finish, he had turned the story into how they had yelled "Black Crow!" during the show. This immediately steered the conversation into an earnest discussion of who was buying beer that night. Then somebody farted, and Stefan cried out: "He who smelt it, dealt it!" And Caroline laughed so hard the milk ran out her nose.

I walked toward home, then changed my mind and walked to the library. I read all the daily reviews for *Julius Caesar*.

Something deathless and dangerous in the world sweeps past you down the darkened aisles at the Mercury Theatre...

Shakespeare himself would have honored and relished it...

Here, splendidly acted and thrillingly produced, is what must certainly be the great Julius Caesar of our time...

Move over and make room for the Mercury Theatre... Brooks Atkinson began, and there followed a nearly unqualified rave.

I didn't know what to feel.

Nobody mentioned my performance. I hadn't really expected they would.

Maybe I should call the theatre, I thought. *Right now*. Maybe there was still time. Maybe Welles had changed his mind....

I headed home. I imagined Cotten pleading with Welles. "Come on, Orson, you *have* to give him the part back. I'm *begging* you, Orson."

"For you, Joe, and only for you...."

When I got home I picked up the phone, but the vital energy to actually dial it seemed to have evaporated. I only stared out the window. A beat-up looking robin was walking carefully along the lawn. Then I dialed Mr. Goldberg at the Rialto Theatre, and I asked if I could come back to work on Saturday.

"Richard," he said, then turned from the phone and sneezed violently. "I'm so glad you called."

Hello, little life.

I sat on my bed and traced my finger along the wings of the eagles printed on the wallpaper. The radio was tuned to Martha Deane. Woolcott Gibbs was the guest. "I've discovered there are two ways of doing Shakespeare," he said. "The old way and the good way. By the old way, I refer to what Tallulah Bankhead is doing over at the Mansfield. By the good way I mean what Orson Welles is doing over at the Mercury."

I switched it off.

"I quit," I told my mother.

"Good."

"I took your advice. I mean, they weren't paying me. They weren't even giving me train money. What did I need that for?"

"You finally made a smart decision. Your father will

be proud of you."

Simply to get out of the house that night, I walked
to the high school.

I sat in the audience, surrounded by somebody else's
parents, and watched *Growing Pains*. Somebody yelled
"Black Crow!" from the audience. Somebody wolf-
whistled at Kristina Stakuna. I felt stuck in an old place,
filled with an old sadness.

I left after the first act.

Then I came home, listened to the radio. At ten
o'clock WEAF broadcast *The First-Nighter* with Les
Tremayne and Barbara Luddy. "Tonight's special guest,"
said the announcer, "is the star of the Mercury Theatre
production of *Julius Caesar*, Orson Welles, in a specially
transcribed broadcast of Anthony Wayne's 'A Late
Edition for Love.'"

Saturday, November 13
Twenty Two

I thought I should at least try to put the pieces of my Westfield life back together. I dressed, grabbed an apple, packed my snare drum in my bike basket, and pedaled down to the fieldhouse on Rahway Avenue. I got there so early the place wasn't open yet, so Korzun, the trumpet player, and I stood outside, and for laughs every time a pretty girl walked by I played a stripper's drum beat, and Korzun played this really lewd warble with his mute—bu*du*budu*wahhwahh!*

It was pretty funny.

The bleachers were wet; the turnout was lousy. The rain and wind had intensified by one o'clock. Umbrellas had been blown inside out. The cheerleaders hid in the fieldhouse until they absolutely had to come out.

Skelly and Stefan were both playing, but football didn't interest me much. It never had. There was a girl on the Plainfield side who looked sort of lonely. She wore a man's hooded plaid raincoat, and I spent most of the game watching her.

Caroline and Kate Rouilliard and all their girlfriends

sat together under their umbrellas. When Westfield finally moved the ball a few yards they all stood up and shouted: ¡*Mucho bueno!*

My shoes were soaked. I could feel the cold rising up through my feet. People were leaving at halftime to listen to the Yale-Princeton game.

Somewhere near the last quarter, I told Korzun that I had a bad headache and had to leave.

"I don't blame you," he said.

I stashed my drum in the fieldhouse, turned up my collar, and bicycled over to the train station.

I knew I was punishing myself, but there I sat, watching the towns roll by, slouched in my seat.

At least the sun was coming out.

I walked up Fifth. There was Saks, Rockefeller Center, the Vanderbilt house.

My sadness seemed to be lifting a little.

Maybe I could write to Welles. Sonja had said I was a writer....

He could still change his mind.

The double-decker buses rode past the embassies; the tourists took pictures of the bronze statue of Atlas.

I ended up at the Metropolitan Museum of Art, back with the mummy cases and the Greek vases and the soft light and the water gurgling through the radiators. I thought about maybe never returning to Westfield High

School.

Somehow a bluebird had flown into the museum, and it was darting wildly around the ceiling. A museum guard stood frozen in the center of the floor with an upraised broom in his hand, staring up at the bird, and for one crazy second it looked to me as if *he* belonged in a museum, as frozen as the Greek vases—*Security Guard with Broom, late 1930s*. I noticed that most of the people in the museum weren't moving either, and it seemed as if the whole museum were an exhibit itself, and all of us, if you could look at this moment with enough distance, were the enchanting curios of some long-dead time: each of us unique, each worth preserving—fabulous mannequins in our stitched shoes and our white shirts and our pocket handkerchiefs. Just the light and the color and the *detail* of it all seemed astonishing.

I sat there, quietly thunderstruck, when the security guard broke his pose and ran on, leaving standing behind him the figure of a pale young woman in a floral-print vest, dark hair in a George Washington. She stepped into the pool of sunlight before me, and the sun glinted off her wire-rim glasses. "So you want to go back to that roast chicken place?" she asked, and she touched her fingers to the small of her neck.

I blinked.

"Gretta?"

"Listen, how on earth you're here today I don't

know," she was saying. "I came here the last couple of days hoping to find you. But, look, I'm standing here like nothing's happened, and I'm about to go through the roof. Look at this. God, I was praying you'd be here." She handed me a business-sized envelope with the *New Yorker*'s return address. Inside was a letter... *Dear Miss Adler: We are pleased to inform you that we have read your short story, "Hungry Generations," and it is very much a story we would like to publish. It's funny and true and touching. We think that with a little work it will truly be—*

I looked up. "A little work?"

"Nothing!" she said. "I called yesterday. A word in; a word out; move a paragraph; nothing major. Of course, if it *was* anything major, I'd do that, too."

"Congratulations," I said.

She was prettier than I remembered.

"Can you believe this?" She took back the letter and read it again. "God, can you believe it? The *New Yorker?* Do you know what this means to me? This is the first real thing I've *ever* had published. And it's all because of you."

"No, it isn't, Gretta."

"You gave it to that girl you knew. Do you honestly think they ever even would have *read* the thing if it just came in over the transom? You did it, Richard. You helped me. I owe you one. God, I don't know how on earth you came here today. I came to thank you and the

Greek vase. Remember? You rubbed the story on the vase!" She laughed.

"Maybe the vase really is lucky."

"Maybe?" Her cheeks were turning rose-colored with excitement. "Everything I write for the rest of my *life* I'm coming here to rub on that vase. Listen, I want to take you to lunch or dinner or whatever the hell time it is now. O.K.?"

"O.K.," I said.

"You know, the last time we were here we had that chicken in the park, and I left and I was thinking to myself: Gretta, here's this guy who loves music like you do, who loves theatre like you do, who loves the radio like you do. Why are you being so damn aloof? You know, not giving you my telephone number and everything. What was I trying to prove? I've been living in the city for half a year, trying to write, trying to meet somebody. My parents are half-crazy I'm not going to college. *A girl with your brains!* I go home—that's all I hear. *A girl with your brains! You're as smart as two colleges on one block! Writing fiction she wants; a big nothing she'll make writing fiction.* And here I meet somebody who's funny and shares the interests I do—and I'm not trying to scare you, don't worry; I'm just talking about friends— but I don't even *say* anything, you know? As if I didn't care. God, what's the *matter* with me?"

I listened while she went on—enjoying her voice,

her passion. I thought: Well, Sonja got this girl's story published. Maybe that was the point of it all. Who knew? That was the intriguing part. No one knew.

Maybe the whole point of it all was to bring Gretta and me together.

"Look, I'm talking a mile a minute," she said. "Tell me about you. Wait, you want to go to that roast chicken place? I'm forcing you, aren't I? You don't really want to."

"I would love to go to that roast chicken place," I said.

"How's the acting?"

"I've given up acting," I said. "Now I'm going to be a writer."

"A writer!" she laughed. "*A guy with your brains!*"

"I'm writing a book about Orson Welles."

"Yeah?"

"I've got this great title: *Talent Only.*"

She considered it a second. "I don't get it. But, hey, now I can help get *you* published!"

"That's an interesting proposition."

"I mean, I *know* somebody at the *New Yorker* now. A real editor. And she's *wonderful*. So you wouldn't have to send a story to just 'the editor' anymore. In fact, I could submit it for you! You know, I could even *recommend* you."

"Recommend me? And you've never read a word I've written?"

"Why the hell not?" she said. "You look pretty talented to me."

"You're not too bad looking yourself."

We were heading out the main door when a voice came shouting down the hall. *"Hold the doors! Hold the doors!"* Gretta held open the inner door; I held open the outer. There was a clatter of footsteps, and the three guards holding brooms aloft came tearing across the floor chasing the bluebird.

The bird made a beeline for the sunlight ahead and soared over us—out into the day and the open sky.

"Hooray for the bird!" cried Gretta.

"I'm glad it didn't hurt itself," said the guard.

Gretta and I and the guards stood on the steps of the museum, and we watched the bird disappear into that late afternoon light. I looked around and saw we were all smiling.

"Wouldn't this make a great ending to a novel?" she asked.

She looked beautiful.